FIGHTING THE FANATICS

A SPECULATIVE FICTION NOVELLA

THE NEXT HIGH PRIEST
BOOK 6

PETER DEHAAN

- Copyeditor: Robyn Mulder
- Cover design: Fanderclai Design
- Author photo: Chelsie Jensen Photography

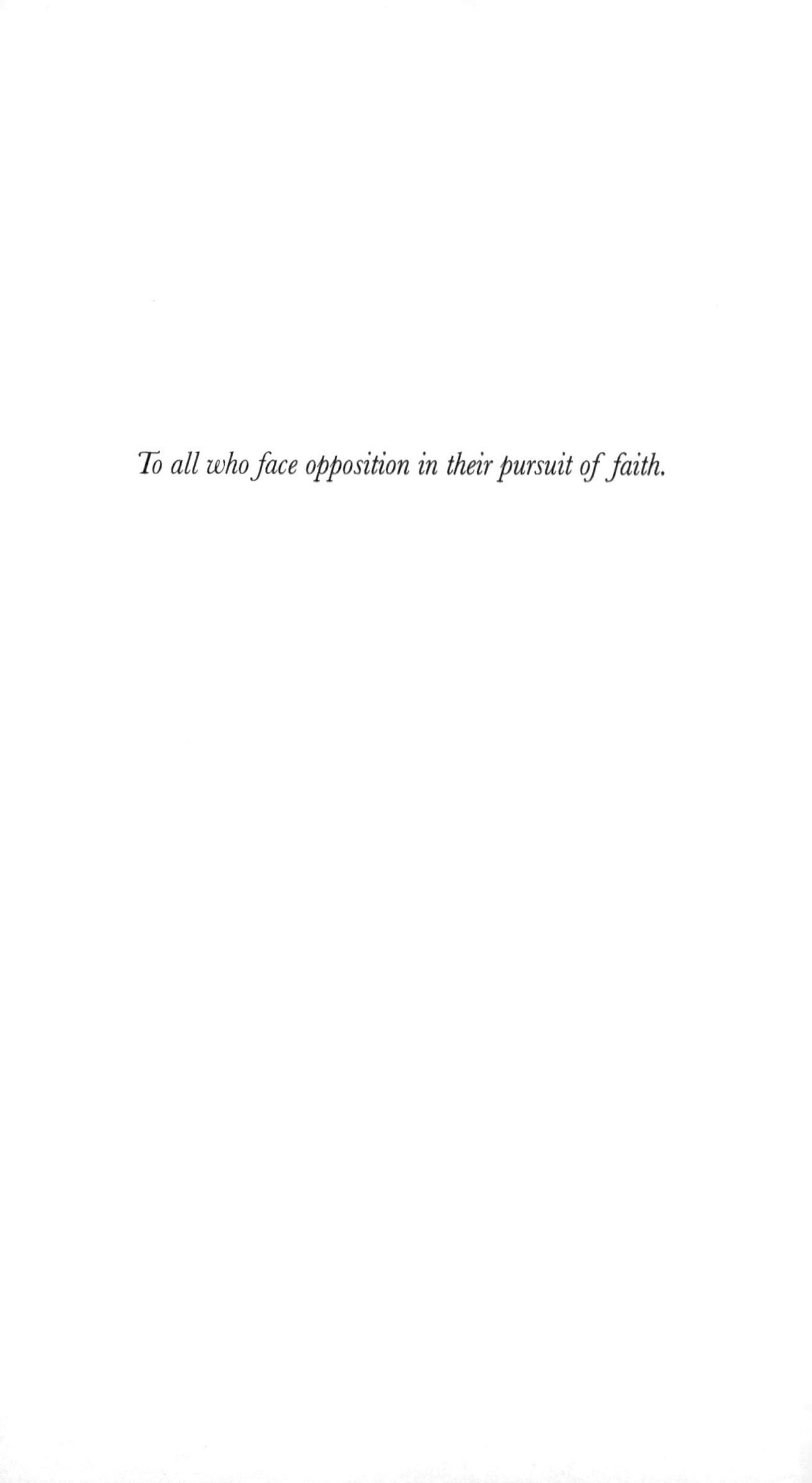

To all who face opposition in their pursuit of faith.

CONTENTS

FIGHTING THE FANATICS

In a world just like ours . . . only different.

The people mock what they do not understand; they oppose my teaching, which stings their ears. A thousand woes upon them, for they are not my children; they do not walk in my light but parade in the darkness of evil. -Prophecy 127.93

1
___

BACK TO NORMAL?

At noon, Emma trudged off to lunch, an uncharacteristic scowl on her face. School had not gone well—not at all. The comfortable rhythm she, Chloe, and Joshua enjoyed had evaporated with the addition of Lane and Kayla. It was sure to get worse when her remaining eight disciples joined them later in the week.

School had taken longer than usual, and Emma had to rush through her assignments to finish by lunch.

Was adding my friends a bad idea? How can I fix this?

Shuffling along with her was Chloe on her right and Joshua on her left. Lane and Kayla held back, likely sensing they were the reason school had gone so poorly.

Already holding her boyfriend's hand, Emma reached out to clasp Chloe's. "Sovereign Lord," she prayed, "please show us how to move forward with school. Fill us with your peace and give me insight in all I do this afternoon. I ask this for your honor and your kingdom."

Her friends agreed in unison. "Amen." The three of them walked in silence the rest of the way to the cafeteria.

Mechanically, Emma piled food on her tray in the food line and joined her team for their regular working lunch. They were all waiting. Emma tried to shove aside her frustration over the morning to embrace the potential of the afternoon.

She sat down but didn't eat. Instead, she made eye contact with each person. She needed to get their attention before she shared from her heart.

"I so value each one of you and all you do to serve the Sovereign and help me. I don't thank you often enough. Sorry."

"Emma," her dad said, "you do a great job at communicating your appreciation." He paused and looked intently into her eyes. "What's wrong?"

"School was a bit frustrating this morning."

Emma blinked back tears. "I'm trying to push that behind me to focus on you and our work here." She took in a slow breath as she reoriented herself. "I've not heard any updates for a few days. Let's do a lightning round. Who wants to go first?"

With hesitation, her dad raised his hand a few inches. It looked funny, but she suppressed her laughter. Instead, she nodded.

"Everything at the health clinic is exceeding my expectations. We've addressed the backlog of staff healthcare concerns and now have extra time. I suggest expanding the clinic to include the priests too."

Fred, her executive administrator, chimed in. "The healthcare coverage the priests have is the best money can buy. We can slash costs in half if we move them to a more typical coverage. The clinic can address what the new plan doesn't cover."

"I've run the numbers," Topher added, "and we'll save enough on the priests' insurance to add coverage for all the staff."

"Everyone agree?" Emma scanned her team. "Let's do it. How long will it take?"

Fred glanced at Emma's father.

"We're ready anytime," her dad confirmed.

"The smoothest transition," Fred said, "will be

to start the beginning of next month. I'll make it happen."

Emma glanced at Christopher, who oversaw human resources. "I've completed doing the competitive wage analysis," he said, "and recommend moving forward with phase one of staff raises. It will mean moving everyone from minimum wage to a higher base. Then, in phase two, we can begin moving individual staff to their competitive level."

Emma's eyes darted to their accountant. "I ran the numbers on that too," Topher said. "I agree we can move forward on phase one with no problem. It will be sustainable."

Emma nodded. "Let's do it," she said to Christopher.

Topher continued his update. "A massive flood of donations came in over the weekend while you were securing the release of the prisoners. It's a record by far and nearly overwhelmed our servers. Anyway, we should be able to move forward with your plans to renovate the old dorm rooms and reopen the Temple school. I recommend we allocate those funds toward that purpose. I'll work on getting repair estimates."

That's when Mark interjected. "Another area

needing capital improvements is the ancient Temple. Ezra is working on some exciting ideas."

Emma sighed. "And I was hoping to renovate the old auditorium."

"Toward what end?" Fred asked.

Emma shrugged. "Not sure. But the Sovereign told me to get it ready to put back into service—soon."

"It would be unwise to pursue all three projects at once," Fred said. "Let's contemplate this and revisit it tomorrow."

Everyone agreed, and all but Emma left to return to work.

Emma remained seated. She pushed her tray of untouched food aside and lowered her forehead to rest on the table. She knew she should be happy—overjoyed, actually—for all the forward progress on the Temple reforms she was spearheading, but she wasn't. At this moment, it all overwhelmed her. She tried to pray but couldn't even focus enough to do that.

That's when Barney cleared his throat. During the whole lunch, her aide had stood in the periphery, available if she needed him to do anything. His emotional support dog, Montgomery, snuggled around his shoe.

Emma sat up with a start.

"Mr. Hernandez approaches, High Priestess. I suspect he has an update."

Emma stood to welcome Hernandez but almost toppled.

"Perhaps you should eat something," Barney advised.

She sat and chomped into a roll as she motioned for Hernandez to join her.

But before he did, he looked at Barney. "I have a personal update for Emma," he said. "Will you please give us privacy?"

Barney scowled but said nothing. With a huff, he turned and marched away, parking himself at the far end of the cafeteria where he could watch Emma.

Hernandez sat across from her. He leaned forward. "You'll never believe what I found on my jacket when we got back on Sunday," he whispered. He pulled a small vial from his pocket, sheltered in his hands so only Emma could see.

A small device lay on the bottom of the container.

"What is it?"

"It's an electronic listening device. Someone was eavesdropping on everything I said the entire trip."

Emma gasped. "Who'd do such a thing?"

2

ONE BUG, TWO HIRES, AND SEVEN PRIESTS

Hernandez shrugged. "Not sure. Maybe Barney Clark. Do you remember last Friday when I updated you on the status of the investigations? Barney acted suspiciously afterward when we went inside the diner. I wonder if he heard everything we said."

"So he knows about the investigation and that he could be arrested?"

"Possibly. But I'm only speculating he was the one who planted the bug on me." Hernandez nodded at the device in the vial.

Emma gasped and leaned forward. "Is he listening to us now?" she whispered.

Hernandez shook his head. "It picks up audio waves, so as long as it's sealed in the vial, we're safe.

But I'd like to do a little test. Do you have eyes on him?"

Emma glanced over Hernandez's shoulder. "He's staring at us."

"Good," Hernandez said. "I'm going to shake the vile, which will generate sound waves inside it. If he's listening, it should create quite a ruckus for him. Watch for any reaction."

"He has his hand up to his ear," Emma said. "I think he's trying to listen."

Hernandez shook the vial with vigor and the device bounced around inside like a ping-pong ball.

Barney jumped, waking Montgomery from a peaceful nap. The man jerked something from his ear and scowled.

"He reacted," Emma said. "He's rubbing his ear. I think he's in pain."

"Although it proves nothing, this all but confirms it in my mind," Hernandez said. "If he heard what we said on Friday, that gave him three days—almost four—to pay off the four guards. I suspect this case will also fall apart, just like the first one."

"Should we confront him?"

Hernandez shrugged. "We have nothing to lose. Call him back."

Emma waved for Barney to return.

When he arrived, Hernandez motioned for him to sit. That's when Hernandez revealed the vial in his hands. He uncapped the lid and dumped the device out.

Remorse covered Barney's face. "Please forgive me, Emma. I want to do better. I'm really trying, but it's hard. Sometimes I stumble." He tipped his head down and brought his hand to his forehead.

"I'm trying to trust you," Emma said. "But you're making it very hard."

"I, however, have no intention of ever trusting you," Hernandez said. He stood and marched away.

Barney held up his hand, palm facing Emma. "I pledge to do better from now on. I promise."

"Should I place you on probation or just fire you?"

As the two of them locked eyes, Fred approached. "I hope I'm not interrupting, but I felt the Sovereign urging me to deliver this right away." He held up a bundle of papers that looked official.

Barney snorted. "Let me guess. It's something I'm not privy to." He stood and stomped off, retreating to the far side of the cafeteria.

"Lynn completed the legal agreement you

requested to allow priests to return their questionable bonuses without fear of reprisal or prosecution," Fred said. "It's ready when you need it."

"We need it now," Emma said. "I found out there are seven priests who want to return their bonuses."

Fred's eyebrows rose. "Once again, you've proven your ability to listen to the Sovereign."

"What's the next step?" Emma asked. "Do we give it to all seven priests or just Gavin? He's the one who contacted me."

"We can schedule a meeting with all the priests and have Lynn review the agreement with them. She can answer their questions, and they can sign it if they want to move forward."

"How soon?" Emma asked.

Fred checked his schedule. "I see no reason we can't do it at three. I'll make it happen. Let's meet in the conference room in the Temple Palace."

While Emma gobbled her lunch, Fred worked his phone to communicate the plan with Lynn and the priests. Her food was cold, but she ate it anyway.

Emma finished her meal just as Fred put away his phone. "I've made all the arrangements. We're good to go."

After Emma took care of her tray, the pair walked to the palace. As always, Barney trailed behind, with Montgomery trotting at his side.

"Two things," Emma said to Fred. "First, I got excited and hired Mrs. Butler to work here at the Temple. She'll teach the Holy Text at the Temple school and give classes for the people. Plus, she'll hold a class for me and my friends." Emma hung her head. "Sorry I didn't discuss it with you first."

"You're correct that we should first discuss hiring situations before you make a commitment, but this time, it isn't a problem. However, please make sure this is an isolated instance."

Emma perked up. "Will do! Thank you for offering me grace."

"What's the other item?" Fred asked.

"I'd like to offer Hernandez a position to head up our security team here on the Temple grounds. The police force suspended him, and I suspect they'll soon fire him. Even if they don't, he'll probably quit anyway."

"That's an excellent idea," Fred said. "Our four guards can't cover the full week without working overtime and could use some extra help. In addition, I struggle to know how to properly manage them. I'd be happy to hand that responsibility over to someone who knows what he's doing."

"Great!" Emma pulled out her phone. "I'll text him right away."

Fred held up his hand. "I should first apprise Topher of both hires so he can plan for the financial aspects. We need to keep Christopher in the loop too. Once I've accomplished both tasks, then you can text him."

"Sorry. These things are always more complicated than I realize. I still have a lot to learn."

"Don't be so hard on yourself," Fred said. "I appreciate your zeal. It's one of your many outstanding characteristics. Just be aware that you have a team around you to help you move forward —the right way. We're not here to restrict you but to facilitate your vision in the way that best honors the Sovereign."

Emma looked up at the portly priest, full of appreciation. "Thank you. Sometimes I wonder how you put up with me."

"Not a problem," he answered. "It's my joy to be of service to you and help grow the Sovereign's kingdom."

When they got to the palace, Fred left to complete preparations for their meeting. Emma went to the conference room. She planned to spend time praying and talking with the Sovereign before meeting with the seven priests.

Barney sat at the end of the conference room table and pulled out his copy of the Holy Text. His actions continued to confound Emma. He was certainly an enigma.

A little before three, the seven priests strolled in, led by Gavin. Each one cast a glaring look at Barney. He rose and repositioned himself in the far corner of the room. Montgomery looked up to watch his master walk away. Then he sauntered over to Emma and curled up at her feet. With a contented sigh, he laid his head on her shoe and closed his eyes.

At one minute before three, Fred and Lynn arrived. They passed out a packet of documents to each priest. Lynn carefully explained each paragraph to them, patiently answering their questions along the way.

When she completed the last paragraph on the last page, Gavin looked up with a relieved expression. "I'm ready to sign."

"I recommend you have your personal attorney review it first," Lynn advised.

"I don't have an attorney—none of us do—and

you explained it thoroughly. We just want to sign, give the money back, and be done with it."

By 4:30, all seven priests had signed their documents and transferred their questionable bonus money back to the Temple account.

That's when Emma noticed Barney fidgeting in the corner. *I sure wish I knew what he was thinking—or scheming.*

3

PROTESTING

E mma embraced the new day, showering quickly. This was in part because of her excitement at eating breakfast with the priests, but also because her too-small shower stall confronted her claustrophobia. She needed to get in and out as fast as possible. Her heart thumped the entire time; she tumbled out to gulp in a lungful of relief.

When ready for the day, she dashed to the cafeteria with a bounce in each step, a smile beaming from her face. These guys—yes, they were all guys—were her people. She so enjoyed eating with them each morning.

They didn't posture before her. They were

themselves: joking, bad manners, and burping to prove it. Yet, they could turn serious in a moment if needed. When Emma finished eating, she stood to give them their blessing for the day, something she did every morning and which they greatly appreciated.

First, she had a request to make. "Not a rush, but please let me know of any passages in the Holy Text that say priests must be men. Everything I've found seems to relate to specific situations in the past, but I'd like to know your thoughts for today."

They nodded with enthusiasm. Given their past performance, she expected her answer before the day was over. After blessing them, she waved goodbye and headed off for school, which now met in the old Temple school building. Though her classroom was in fine shape, the rest of the rooms needed a good cleaning, and all the dorm rooms needed a complete overhaul before she could reopen the Temple school. She could hardly wait till that day came.

Her enthusiasm for the day waned, however, as she neared the building. She heard men chanting. Though she couldn't make out their words, their tone sounded angry. When Emma rounded the corner, the sight of ten priests holding a protest confirmed what was happening.

They were all part of Alpha group, the ten priests whose spirits lacked the light of the Sovereign living within them, the ten priests who had received significant, unsanctioned—and possibly illegal—bonuses over the years.

Two of them carried signs with her likeness, which looked like her unflattering seventh grade yearbook picture. It was possibly the very worst photo of her, taken on perhaps her worst day ever. Her image had a red circle around it and a diagonal line through it.

Other priests carried signs with hurtful language directed at her: heretic, thief, and traitor.

Each man wore his priestly robe. With their cowls raised, it made them look sacred, even though Emma knew better. They chanted, "Emma Barlow is not our High Priest. Emma Barlow is not *your* High Priest. Restore our traditions. Do it now."

Sovereign, help me, Emma prayed silently.

She rolled her shoulders back and held her head high. She slowed her pace and tried to look approachable. As she neared them, she forced a smile. "Can we talk about it?"

The priests responded by chanting louder. She tried again. They ignored her. "Maybe after school we can talk," she said as loudly as she could without screaming. With heart thumping, she scooted into the building and headed to class. Even inside her classroom, she could still hear their low rumble. It was going to be hard to concentrate.

Though school wouldn't start for another fifteen minutes, Joshua and Chloe were already there, along with Lane and Kayla. Three more of her disciples had joined them this morning. They looked tense.

"We didn't feel safe at public school anymore," William said. "But with those fanatics protesting outside, I'm not sure this is much better. Maybe we don't belong here."

"No worries," Emma said. "It's not normally like this. Those ten priests have been giving me grief since I got here. But the others are all on my side. The staff too. With the Sovereign's help, I'll fix this. Then we won't have any reason to worry."

Jennifer stood and cleared her throat. "Since you're all here, let's get started. I want to explain how we'll be handling your schooling. Initially, I acted as proxy for Emma's parents to homeschool her. Then we added Joshua and Chloe, whom I treated the same way."

Jennifer scanned the students before continuing. "But to be effective as our numbers grow, we need to shift into a self-paced classroom environment. Each morning, I'll provide a structure for you to study and complete your assignments on your own. After lunch, those needing more time or individual instruction should return. Once each person finishes their work for the day, they'll be dismissed. The key is to not rush through your assignments just to finish with your classmates. We each learn and work at our own pace. Let us embrace that reality."

Emma raised her hand. "May we still work in groups?"

Jennifer smiled. "Good question. As for now, I will allow it, so long as you don't distract other students."

Emma nodded. That meant she, Joshua, and Chloe could still work together and help each other with their lessons. It also meant that things would get mostly back to the way they were before her other disciples had joined their little school.

They pushed through the day. As Emma worked

on algebra, her phone vibrated. She had forgotten to silence it; the priests' protest must have distracted her. She glanced up at Jennifer, who'd also heard the phone reverberating on the desktop. "Sorry," Emma mouthed to her teacher.

Jennifer tipped her head down, which Emma received as permission to read the message. It was from Scarlett: *Though I don't want to, I've been assigned to cover the protesters at the palace. So sorry. Maybe we can do a follow-up piece this afternoon?*

Emma typed a quick response. *Sounds good. Let's talk after lunch.* Then she turned her phone off and pushed it aside. Jennifer confirmed her approval with a nod.

Emma worked diligently through her assignments and completed them first. She gave them to Jennifer and left without waiting for Joshua and Chloe. She didn't want them to have to deal with whatever she would encounter when she walked outside.

The protest of ten was now down to five. They marched in silence. She assumed that once Scarlett had interviewed the protesters, five of them took a break while the other five continued. They'd likely switch off throughout the day. As she approached, they resumed chanting, "Emma Barlow is not our

High Priest. Emma Barlow is not *your* High Priest. Restore our traditions. Do it now."

"Can we talk about it?" Emma asked the remaining five as they marched past her. Like before, they responded by chanting louder. She shook her head and left.

4

ONE STEP FORWARD AND TWO STEPS BACK

T hough Emma arrived early for lunch, Fred and Mark were already there, waiting for her at their regular table.

Mark spoke first. "As the Chief of Priests, I take full responsibility for the actions of those fanatical priests. I'm sorry I didn't do a better job of containing the situation."

"It's not your fault. It's on me," Emma said. "Has Scarlett's interview aired?"

Fred nodded. "Though she gave them a platform to voice their frustrations, her questions were critical of them and supportive of you. You should take comfort in that."

"Scarlett offered to do a follow-up with me this afternoon," Emma said. "I'd like to do it, but

I'll need to shuffle my schedule a bit." Emma pulled out her phone and texted Scarlett about what time she wanted to meet. They settled on two.

"What are the priests complaining about?" Emma asked Mark. "They won't tell me."

"They have three gripes," Mark said. "First, they claim you're teaching heresy, and it must stop. Second, they say your reforms are ruining our religion. Third, they claim you're stealing money from them and damaging the integrity of the priesthood."

"I tried to talk with them twice—both before school and after," Emma said. "But I don't think they want to talk."

"I agree," Mark said. "They seem more intent on publicity than resolution. I suspect their goal is to force you out. They need to drum up public pressure to make it happen."

"Just in case they're open to talking," Emma said, "let's invite them to a meeting this evening at 7:00."

"I'll extend the invitation," Mark said, "but my expectations are low."

As the rest of Emma's team joined her for their working lunch, she turned their attention to yesterday's tabled topic: which capital project to focus on first.

"Last night I walked through the old auditorium, as well as the ancient Temple," Emma said. "The auditorium looks to be in good shape overall. The mechanical systems seem in fine working order, and I don't see the need for any renovations. I think a thorough cleaning is what it needs. Our existing staff should be able to handle it."

"I agree," Christopher said. "Since we eliminated maid service, we now have more staff than work for them to do. This would be an ideal task for them."

Emma continued. "Second, we already know the dorm rooms in the Temple school need a complete renovation.

"As far as the ancient Temple, it needs some repairs, and electricity and fire suppression without detracting from the historical nature of the building. We also need to provide restroom facilities and not use portable units."

Everyone looked at her in shock. Fred broke their silence. "Though we respect your opinion, we need a professional to make these determinations. You're not an architect or an engineer."

"I agree," Emma said. "You're so right, but

before I came here, I planned to become an architect and was studying to do so."

"I wasn't aware they taught architecture in high school," Fred said.

"They don't," Emma answered. "I was studying on my own in the evenings. I even completed a couple of online classes for college credit. But then I became more interested in reading the Holy Text. That's when seeking the Sovereign became more important than studying architecture. And now I'm here."

"This shouldn't surprise me at all," Fred said, "but, nevertheless, it does."

"Let's work on the old auditorium first," Emma said, "the ancient Temple next, and the dorm rooms last."

"Based on Emma's preliminary determination, and with the understanding we'll need professional confirmation, I agree," Fred said.

Everyone looked at Topher. "I've allocated the donations received over the weekend and the bonuses the priests returned yesterday to a special fund to address renovations on the Temple grounds. I see no reason we can't move forward."

Though Emma wanted to confirm their decision, she felt she should let Fred do it. She turned toward him.

Fred scanned the group and then concluded, "I think we're all in agreement. I'll schedule a professional analysis. But as we wait for the determination, let's have our staff begin the cleaning process."

This excited Emma to no end. But then she remembered the protesting priests and her interview in an hour with Scarlett.

Emma sighed. *One step forward and two steps back.*

5

INTERVIEWED AND SURPRISED

Emma waited in a small meeting room in the palace, next to what would one day be her office. She spent time with the Sovereign as she waited for Scarlett to arrive. Though she didn't know what to expect for their interview, she felt ready. The Sovereign filled her with peace.

When Scarlett arrived, her demeanor seemed guarded. She gave Emma a stiff hug and whispered in her ear. "My boss didn't like my tone when I interviewed the priests. She told me to not go easy on you today. I'm sorry."

Appreciative for the warning, this news deflated Emma's enthusiasm for the interview. Her pulse quickened. She focused on controlling her breathing as she prayed for the Sovereign's leading in what to say and how to phrase it.

In no time at all, they were ready to begin. The cameraman gave Scarlett her cue.

"This is Scarlett Steele with Xtend News Network. I'm sitting with the High Priestess to get her response to the serious allegations the priests have made against her. Emma, what do you have to say to their charges?"

"I respect their right to protest and voice their opinions. But they won't tell me what they're mad about. What I can say is that in my short time here as High Priestess, my only goal has been to honor the Sovereign. A key way to do that is for everything we do to align with what the Holy Text says, to move away from our traditions and more fully embrace Scripture."

"How do you react to the charge of heresy?"

Emma relaxed. She had a ready answer. "My mentor Gabe tells me that one person's heresy is another person's orthodoxy. Disagreements are normal. I study the Holy Text for a couple of hours most every night. Ask them how much time they spend reading it. I expect little to none. Anyway, everything I do follows what Scripture says. The other thirty-eight priests study the Text to confirm what I read."

"They also claim your many reforms are hurting our religion," Scarlett said. "Given the rapid changes you've made, how can you dispute that?"

"I understand why they're concerned," Emma said, "but I disagree with them. It's normal for people to not like change. Frederick Mitchell, my executive admin, tells me that change is opposed, change is viewed as loss, and change is mourned."

"That makes sense," Scarlett said, "but aren't all these changes attacking our practices?"

"The changes I'm making better align our practices with Scripture. Only these ten priests disagree. I have the full support of all the others."

"But what about the Sunday services?"

"On Sundays we're making changes in a slow, careful way. We explain what we'll do and why. We give the people time to process it. Then we implement it. We now have ten times the number of people here each week. Doesn't that prove most people like what I'm doing? If you're in town this Sunday, please join us at either 9:30 or 11:00." Emma relaxed her frame, looked into the camera, and smiled. "Everyone's invited."

"I'll be there!" Scarlett promised. "But what about the charges that you're stealing their money? That's a serious allegation. They say you slashed their pay and took away their healthcare coverage."

Emma laughed. "That's certainly an interesting slant. These ten priests once enjoyed a very generous but unapproved—possibly illegal—bonus program. We put a stop to that. They've each received millions over the years, so don't feel sorry for them for a moment.

"As far as taking away their healthcare coverage, that is incorrect. We're planning to move them from their expensive deluxe policy to a more normal plan, like most everyone else has. We'll cover any shortfall with our healthcare clinic, which we just reopened."

"They claim you only pay them minimum wage. I have proof. What do you say to that?"

"We do indeed pay them minimum wage for forty hours a week. Yet they do no work. They also receive a stipend for personal expenses. Plus they have a pension plan. And don't forget that we give them a place to stay and food to eat. We even give them free haircuts."

Scarlett frowned. "What do you mean the priests do no work?"

"When I got here," Emma said, "I found out that aside from one shift a week working in the ancient Temple, none of the priests did any work. They expected the staff to wait on them: clean their rooms, do their laundry, and deliver their meals. I stopped that. Most of the priests embraced this change and were glad for it. They're now doing work that they're passionate about and that interests them. They're getting so much done. Yet these ten priests who are protesting have opposed all this."

"What do they do all day?" Scarlett asked.

"Aside from protesting . . . and opposing my reforms . . . nothing. They don't even take a shift at the ancient Temple anymore. Ezra and his team have that covered. One of the staff here told me that some of these priests are serious gamers, others spend all day watching TV, and a few just read."

Emma continued. "Compare this to the staff who also got minimum wage, were forced to donate their overtime hours, and had to work seven days a week. They didn't even have healthcare coverage. Fixing this is my highest concern. We've already addressed most of it and are working on the rest."

"I understand this isn't the first protest here on the Temple grounds," Scarlett said. "Just a few weeks ago, the staff held their own protest. Some see this as an alarming trend. What do you have to say about that?"

"The staff was protesting all the problems I just mentioned. I agreed with them and tried to join their protest . . . until a guard stopped me and locked me in my room for several days. Once I got free, I began working to address their concerns. Ask any of them, and I'm sure they'll say they're pleased with the progress."

"As for the priests protesting, you already admitted you haven't talked with them. Aren't you being unfair?"

"I tried to talk with them twice this morning," Emma said, "but they just chanted me down. I also had a meeting scheduled last Thursday to discuss things here at the Temple, but none of these ten priests showed up. We've also invited them to a meeting tonight at seven. If they want to talk, they'll have another chance then."

"Thank you, Emma, for sharing your side of this developing story. As always, we appreciate hearing your perspective." Scarlett looked directly at the camera. "Stay tuned. We'll keep you posted."

The red light on the camera went out, and the cameraman hefted it off his shoulder.

Both Emma and Scarlett sighed, long and relieved.

Scarlett brushed at her eye. "I'm so sorry I had to ask you those questions. If it makes any difference, know that I'm on your side."

"We're all good," Emma said.

As Scarlett left, she turned toward Emma. "See you tonight at seven!"

Emma groaned.

6

SEVEN O'CLOCK

After supper, Emma entered the palace through the servant's entrance in the back. Verifying everything was ready in the large conference room, she made her way to the front entrance of the palace.

The Xtend News Network van, along with Scarlett and her cameraman, were already there. Emma went outside to greet them.

"Sorry about the interview this afternoon," Scarlett whispered to Emma. "I got in trouble for that one too. My boss told me I should've pivoted once I realized the protesters were lying. But I was just doing what she told me."

"From now on," Emma said, "maybe you should just go with your gut."

"That's wise advice."

"You may talk with the priests before and after the meeting," Emma said. "But please wait outside and give us privacy as we meet."

"Mr. Clark already stated that, but I was hoping you might allow us access."

"Having you wait outside was my idea," Emma said.

"Got it. May I record some comments from you to open our coverage? This won't be live; I'll edit the piece once I talk with everyone involved."

As Scarlett picked up her microphone, the cameraman hoisted the camera to his shoulder. He signaled Scarlett to begin. "Scarlett Steele here with the High Priestess, Emma Barlow, before tonight's anticipated meeting with the dissident priests, whom some are calling fanatics. Emma, what do you hope to accomplish in tonight's meeting?"

"It's quite simple. I just want to learn about their concerns. I'm sure there's a way to fix them, but I need to know what the issues are first."

Scarlett lowered her microphone and the record light on the camera went out. Scarlett leaned toward Emma and whispered, "Perhaps we can talk again after the meeting."

Before Emma could answer, ten smiling priests

strode up to the palace and diverted Scarlett's attention. Emma retreated inside, but not before hearing one priest tell Scarlett, "We're most excited about meeting with the High Priestess tonight. We hope she's finally willing to listen to our concerns."

Once inside, Emma passed a security guard headed toward the front entrance. "I'll be stationed outside throughout the meeting," he said. "Another guard will be outside the conference room—just in case."

Emma nodded her appreciation and strode to the conference room. Fred was already there with an armful of papers, along with Mark. Emma would open the meeting, Mark would talk about the bonuses, and Fred was there for support as needed.

The priests filed into the conference room and squeezed on one side of the table, across from Emma and the two men. She encouraged them to spread out and sit around the table, but they ignored her. As each one sat, he pulled out his phone and stared at the screen, as if nothing else mattered. Stoic frowns replaced their earlier smiles.

"Since we're all here," Emma said, "let's get started." The priests remained fixated on their phones, their fingers moving over the screens, as if they were all texting.

Emma tried again. "To get started, I'd like to hear your concerns. Who wants to go first?"

No one looked up. They all continued typing.

"I was hoping to have a discussion tonight," Emma continued, "but if no one wants to talk, that will be hard. I guess I'll open, and you can give me your input."

They continued working their phones.

"We've made a lot of changes here at the palace that affect the priests. Most priests support this and are excited about the improvements. You are not. But I want to give you time to process everything. I hope you'll one day see these as positive developments."

The only people looking at Emma were Mark and Fred, their mouths agape and their eyes open wide.

Emma pressed on. "Since you're not willing to talk, and I'm not even sure you're listening, let me pull the bandage off and be done with it." Her anger rose. "Starting tomorrow, your maid service and laundry service will stop. So will getting shaves and beard trims at the salon. And you'll now eat all your meals in the cafeteria and not just some.

"Everything that currently applies to the rest of the priests now applies to you too."

Emma considered if she should say more. "As you've heard, we're rightsizing your healthcare plans starting next month. So use the clinic for all your non-emergency healthcare needs. Your pay and pension stay the same. And you've already heard that the unauthorized—and possibly illegal—bonus program has been terminated."

As Fred passed out the papers Lynn had drawn up, Emma continued. "Seven of the priests have already returned the unethical bonus money they received. I'd like you to follow their example. The rest of the priests received no bonuses, so you ten are the holdouts. This agreement will allow you to return the money and avoid punishment, prosecution, and prison time."

"But it's a limited time offer," Fred added. "Anyone who wants to learn more can schedule a meeting with me and Mark tomorrow afternoon. Lynn, our attorney, will be here to explain each paragraph."

Not one priest picked up their document or even glanced at it, but their fingers flew over their phones with more vigor.

"Does anyone have any questions? Comments?" Mark asked. "Otherwise, it looks like this will be a very short meeting."

The priests also ignored Mark, just as they had Emma and Fred.

Mark's normally calm demeanor gave way to frustration. "A last item is that we expect you to begin working here at the Temple. Forty hours a week—no less. And with a positive attitude, or else I'll have no choice but to terminate you. You have until the end of this week to decide what you're going to do."

Mark stood and stomped out the door.

The ten priests stood and marched out the other door.

Emma looked at Fred, and he shook his head. "I don't think that could've gone any worse."

7

———

VINDICATION

Now it was Emma's turn to shake her head. "Don't say that. I still need to talk to Scarlett. She wants to do a concluding interview with me."

Wide-eyed, Fred followed Emma outside, leaving the conference room, with seven copies of the bonus agreement still sitting on the table.

Scarlett strode up to Emma with microphone in hand. The cameraman positioned himself to record everything. "Emma, the priests told me you refused to listen to their concerns or even talk with them. That you just yelled. What happened?"

"I'm afraid they gave you bad information—again," Emma said, as calmly as she could, given that anger roiled within her after how poorly the priests had treated her. *Fill me with peace*, she prayed silently. *Calm my emotions.*

Emma relaxed and smiled at Scarlett. "What really happened was just the opposite. The priests would not talk to us or even make eye contact. Not one of them said a single thing the entire meeting."

"But it's their word against yours," Scarlett said. "Ten against one. Who should we believe?"

Fred moved to Emma's right side while the security guard hovered on her left.

"Who do you trust to tell you the truth?" Emma asked Scarlett.

Fred held up his phone. "I recorded the entire meeting. I have proof of who's telling the truth and who's lying. Aside from Emma, only Mark and I spoke. The ten priests said nothing. Absolutely nothing."

Scarlett lowered her mic, and the cameraman stopped taping. The reporter listened to the four-minute recording. "Though you came down hard on them," Scarlett concluded, "I certainly under-stand why. The important thing is that this recording proves the priests lied. My coverage will confirm that."

8

GABE

On Thursday morning, the priests resumed their protest in front of the Temple school building. Emma entered through the building's rear door to avoid them, but she could still hear their angry chants filling the air. Chloe waited for her inside.

As they walked down the corridor to their classroom, Chloe whispered to Emma, "If we get done with school in time, could you help me talk with Gabe? I think he's avoiding me."

"That doesn't sound like him," Emma said. "No worries. After school, we'll track him down."

"Thanks." Chloe tipped her head into Emma's shoulder. "You're the best."

Joining them at school today sat the rest of

Emma's disciples. All twelve of them were now here.

Jennifer scanned the growing number of students. "Instead of having a modified homeschool, it's morphing into a microschool. We'll adjust accordingly." She reiterated what she had said on Wednesday about how each day would proceed. "With thirteen of you," she said with a smile, "I guess I'm going to need to record attendance."

Each new student told her their name as she jotted it down. Then they all went to work.

By eleven, Emma had finished her lessons for the day. She waited for Chloe to finish hers. The girls turned in their assignments and left. As usual, Barney, along with Montgomery, trailed behind them.

The chants of the priests' protest filled the air. "Emma Barlow is not our High Priest. Emma Barlow is not *your* High Priest. Restore our traditions. Do it now."

Emma sighed. *Will they ever stop?*

She pulled out her phone and texted Gabe: *Where are you?*

His response came quickly: *I'm waiting for you in your future office in the palace.*

Chloe looked at Emma with confusion. "It's like he's expecting you."

"I suspect the Sovereign prompted him," Emma said. "With Gabe, that often happens. He's most amazing."

When they arrived, Barney waited outside the office while Emma and Chloe walked inside. Montgomery bounced in behind Emma. Gabe sat at the desk chair with his eyes closed. His lips gyrated as strange words wafted forth. Keeping his eyes closed, he stopped vocalizing. "Welcome, ladies."

The two sat across from him. At last, he opened his eyes.

Emma knew Chloe had never been this close to Gabe. She watched as her friend studied the man she once feared. Now she seemed drawn to him. Chloe asked, "Can you help me better listen to and understand the Divine Spirit?"

"A wise request, indeed." Gabe smiled. "Yet with Emma's excellent tutelage, I perceive you're already mastering it in grand fashion. Fine-tuning this essential skill will require concerted practice."

Chloe leaned forward and peered into Gabe's face. "Your eyes . . . kind of remind me of my dad's." She giggled nervously.

Gabe bent toward her and gave an anxious chuckle. "And your eyes remind me of my son's."

Chloe gasped. Her body froze. "Are you . . . are you . . . my grandfather?"

Gabe tipped his head.

Chloe leapt to her feet and ran around the desk, her arms straining to reach him. "Grandpa!" She wrapped her arms around him and squeezed.

"Bless you, my child. Your presence makes my heart leap with joy. Today is a day I never thought would come, even though the Sovereign promised me it would."

Emma was just as shocked. She chastised herself for not figuring it out sooner. Though Cruz was a common enough last name, she should have suspected a connection. Chloe and Gabe's faces were strikingly similar. Over the past several weeks Gabe had let clues slip before he caught himself. But until now, it never occurred to Emma that her mentor was her best friend's estranged grandfather.

Chloe pulled away from Gabe. "Why didn't you tell me sooner? I've been trying to talk with you for over a week, but you kept ignoring me."

"A restraining order prohibits me from having any contact with you until you turn eighteen. Even then, my son will not be pleased. I risk arrest even being in the same room with you, but it's a chance I'm willing to take. Just to see you one time is worth it to me."

"Does it matter that she approached you?" Emma asked.

"I am unsure of the answer to your insightful query," Gabe said. "Therefore, I beseech you both to keep this unsanctioned interaction a secret. I've already spent enough time incarcerated and wish to avoid any more."

"Dad hasn't told me much about you," Chloe said. "I only know that he wants nothing to do with you and blames you for my mother abandoning us."

Gabe lowered his head and stared at the floor. "Your father's conclusions are not erroneous. I don't fault him for wanting to keep us apart. My steadfast prayer is that he will one day be open to see I am a changed man and accept me back into his life—and yours."

9

BARNEY

The office door opened, and Fred walked in. He stopped short as he scanned the trio. "Am I interrupting something? I thought today might be a good day to clean out this office for Emma's use. As the High Priestess, it is, after all, hers."

Emma suggested Chloe and Gabe retreat to the small meeting room next door. As they left, Barney walked in. "That was a most interesting development."

Emma prayed he'd keep Gabe and Chloe's connection a secret, but she worried he wouldn't.

"I'd like the three of us to work on organizing this office," Fred said. Then he turned to Barney.

"Our first order of business is for you to remove your personal items."

"I have much to gather," Barney said. "The last time I was here was when I was arrested. I'd also like to retrieve my belongings from my old quarters, which I no longer have access to."

"Gabe knew you would one day want your personal items," Fred said. "He organized them and neatly stored them in boxes. We'll get those once we're done here."

Fred and Barney methodically worked through the office, dividing its contents into three categories: items to keep, Barney's personal property, and things to save—for now—just in case. There wasn't much Emma could do, so she played with Montgomery in the corner as she listened to their interaction.

They'd made it through about one third of the office when Fred checked the time. "I'd hoped to finish this before noon, but it's a larger task than I expected. Let's head to lunch and return here with renewed energy."

Setting out for the cafeteria, chants of the fanatical priests' protest reminded Emma of the challenge before her. She sighed, trying to excise the frustration from her being. Then she remembered prayer was the better solution. *Sovereign Lord,* she said silently, *remove the weight of this burden from me and show me what to do.*

As they walked, the two men flanked Emma, with Montgomery at her heels. She enjoyed the energetic pup's presence and appreciated that he wanted to be near her, but with him constantly underfoot, she worried about accidentally stepping on him. She trod with care.

Barney interrupted her thoughts. "My reinstatement agreement says I'm not allowed on Temple grounds over the weekend, but can we make an exception for the Sunday service?"

Wanting to support him on his spiritual journey—meager as it was—Emma had a quick answer. "Yes! That's a great idea."

"But only during the service," Fred clarified. "Do not arrive early, and you must leave once it's over."

"Understood." Barney dipped his head. "Thank you. Both of you."

Fred cleared his throat. "I suspect this will not be news to you, Barney, nor will it come as a surprise, but it will be for Emma. The four guards who agreed to testify against you as the instigator of the threats and attacks on the High Priestess at the high school and here at the Temple grounds have recanted their statements."

Emma suppressed her shock—and her anger. The second attempt to punish Barney and remove him had failed. All that remained was the issue with the priests' bonuses. She hoped that would put him away for good and forever remove him from her presence.

Fred continued. "In other news, although we're still awaiting an official report, the initial feedback on the viability of reopening the old auditorium confirms there are no major issues; it just needs a good cleaning. We're already working on that. Christopher says they plan to have the essential areas done by this weekend and all work finished by the end of next. It will then be ready, Emma, for use when the time comes."

She wondered when that might be.

Once at the cafeteria, they selected their food and joined the rest of Emma's leadership team for their working lunch. Ezra had joined them today.

Mark explained the priest's presence. "Ezra wants to share his initial ideas for the ancient Temple. With your approval, he'll move ahead to get firm quotes and establish a workable timetable."

Mark nodded to Ezra, who cleared his throat and stood.

"There's no need to stand, Ezra," Mark said. "This is an informal time of sharing."

Ezra smiled as he returned to his chair. "I understand Emma has already pointed out that the Temple needs attention for some deferred maintenance issues. I also want to bring in electricity, and we need a fire suppression system. These comprise phase one. I don't think it will take long and expect the cost will be modest—under a hundred thousand.

"Once finished, I recommend we focus our attention on the pilgrims and the tourists who visit the Temple each day. I want to give them a spiritual experience. I also want to reinstate the thrice-daily prayer times we read about in the Holy Text: morning supplication, noontime praise, and evening reflection."

Emma beamed. "Excellent! Great ideas. What else?"

"For phase two, I recommend we construct a nice but modest welcome center next to the Temple. It will be a place for visitor orientation, as well as providing much needed restroom facilities. I'd also like to provide space for a small gift shop and museum to sell and showcase items relating to our faith. This, of course, is a larger project and will take time.

"The preliminary—and I stress, preliminary—estimate is that it will take about four months and cost about 1.5 million."

All eyes turned to Topher. The able accountant leaned back, crossed his arms, and beamed. "The money we've set aside for capital improvements is more than sufficient to handle this. But let's be careful with our expenditures and not get carried away. We still have the renovation of the dorm rooms for the Temple school, and Frederick wants to remodel the lower level of the priests' quarters. It's barely livable as it is."

"Based on my room," Emma said, "I agree with Frederick. Though my room is fine for me, the priests on the lower level deserve a nicer place to live."

After the group gave Ezra approval to move forward and submit a formal plan, everyone left to return to work. Back at Emma's future office, Fred and Barney continued reorganizing, while Emma sat on the floor and happily played with Montgomery. An alert on her phone interrupted her bliss and gave the puppy a start.

Emma stood. "I have a 2 o'clock with Ashley for a trim. It's been a while. Be back soon."

As Emma turned to leave, Barney took a step in her direction.

"You'll just be bored sitting in the salon," Emma said. "Why don't you stay here and work with Frederick? That's the best use of your time."

Barney shifted his gaze from Emma to Fred.

"I concur," Fred said.

Emma walked through the doorway to leave for her appointment. Montgomery followed. She turned back. "Looks like he wants to go with me," she said to Barney. "You mind?"

With gritted teeth, Barney shook his head.

10

ASHLEY

Emma entered Ashley's salon promptly at two. Montgomery scooted in with her, snaking in between and around her feet.

"Oh! Goody," Ashley squealed. "You brought your little buddy with you." The youthful cosmetologist bent down and ruffled Montgomery's fluffy head. "Come here, you little cutie. Let me give you some lovin'."

Emma sat in the salon's lone chair. When Ashley stood after playing with Montgomery, the little pup climbed onto Emma's lap.

"Though I like having him around," Ashley said, "he's going to get in my way sitting there. Wait! Wait just a second. I have an idea." Ashley stepped into a storage room and returned with a large plastic shopping bag. She pulled out a doggy toy and squeezed it twice. Montgomery perked up when he heard it squeak. Ashley tossed the toy to the floor, where it bounced with another squeak. Montgomery sprang from Emma's lap and dove after the toy.

Next, Ashley pulled a small doggy bed out of the bag and placed it in the corner. She playfully tugged the plastic toy from Montgomery's mouth, squeaked it twice, and tossed it onto the bed. Montgomery bounded after it, curled around the toy, and laid his head down. His tail wagged and his eyes fluttered shut.

"I know you like dogs," Emma said, "but why do you have puppy things when you don't have a dog?"

"Now that I'm not working every day and have some free time, I want to get one." Ashley beamed. "I got all the supplies and am just waiting to find the right puppy." Ashley scrutinized Emma's hair. "Looks like you washed it this morning. No need to do it again. Nice and clean. I'll just trim it dry. It would be better for your hair and save us both time. Are you good with that? I'm good with that. Okay then. Let's do it."

Emma stretched out her hand and rested it on Ashley's forearm. "Take a breath. Relax."

"You're right, my Emma. I need to slow down. I need to breathe. No need to be nervous around you. But sometimes I am. Can't stop myself. Okay. Need to breathe. I'll do that. Thanks, my Emma, for the reminder." Ashley closed her eyes and sucked in a deep breath. Then she exhaled slowly and opened her eyes. "Okay, then." She picked up her scissors and snipped the air twice. "Let's do this."

"It's getting long," Emma said. "What do you recommend?"

Ashley had a ready answer. "I think we should trim about three inches off the length and do a bit of layering. That will make it easier for you to manage and not take much work to produce a great look every morning. At least, that's my thoughts. What do you think?"

"Sounds good."

As Ashley worked on Emma's hair, the stylist gushed about all the changes that had happened with the Temple staff since Emma's arrival. "You'll never believe what a difference you've made here. I'm no longer tired. When I leave work, I have plenty of free time. And I again look forward to coming back each morning. You showing up here has been wonderful for us all. Everyone on staff thinks so. Everyone knows so. Thank you. Thank you from the bottom of my heart."

"What about Topher?" Emma asked. "Have you been able to spend much time with him?"

Ashley paused her work and cooed. "For sure. We go out for dinner or do something every night. Each time he looks at me my little heart goes pitter-patter." Ashley patted her chest three times, closed her eyes, and let out a most contended sigh.

When she opened her eyes, she resumed cutting Emma's hair. "Being with him is a delight. Total delight. We're going to get married!" Ashley gasped. "Oops! It's a secret. Wasn't supposed to tell anyone. Please keep it to yourself and pretend I didn't say anything. I know you will. I trust you. It's me I'm worried about."

"Then let me say—unofficially—congratulations!" Emma said. "I'm so happy for you—both of you."

"Want you to perform the ceremony," Ashley said. "Oops! There I go again, saying things I'm not supposed to. Topher's going to ask you. Please act surprised when he does. We're just waiting to save up enough money to get a place of our own. Two months. Three max."

"I can't perform the ceremony," Emma said. "A priest needs to do that."

"Oh, my Emma. Silly Emma. You're the High Priestess. You can most certainly marry us."

"Guess you're right," Emma said. "The thought just surprised me. I'll need to check with Fred on how to make it legal and all. Then I'll need to figure out what to do."

"Keep it simple and short," Ashley said. "We don't have money for a fancy wedding anyway—not that either of us want that."

"Maybe I could do a ceremony like we read about in the Holy Text. Think about that. So will I."

"Sounds good," Ashley said. "I'll tell Topher too. No, I can't do that. If I do, then he'll know I spilled the beans. Oh no! Now I have another secret to keep."

"Without sounding like a parent," Emma said, "are you sure you're not rushing things? You've only been dating for like a week or two."

"So true. Though it's only been a couple of weeks, we've admired each other from afar for over a year. I've been dreaming of marrying him the whole time—since I first arrived—and he's been thinking about me most of that time too. Plus, we've got a few months to get to know each other better as we save up our money."

Ashley handed Emma a mirror. "Ta da!" she said with a graceful flourish of her hands.

Emma ran her fingers through her remaining locks. "It feels great and looks about perfect. Though I won't know for sure until I wash it, I'd say this is the best trim I've ever had."

Emma stood but wondered what to do. She felt she should pay Ashley, but the trim was a benefit of being a Temple employee. Was she? As High Priestess, she guessed she was. Should she leave a tip? Not that she had any money.

"Your appreciation is all the payment I need. In fact, it's more than enough," Ashley said as Emma fumbled awkwardly. "Thank you for the opportunity to serve you."

"And thank you for your service."

"And don't forget, me and Topher getting married is top secret. When he asks you to do the ceremony, try to act surprised."

"No worries," Emma said. "We're good."

11

CLARITY

As Emma and Montgomery returned to her future office in the palace, she tried to tune out the chants of the protesting priests. One phrase grated at her: "Emma Barlow is not our High Priest."

The words echoed in her head: "Emma Barlow is not our High Priest." Even when the zealots chanted something else, even amid the lulls in between, what Emma heard over and over was "Emma Barlow is not our High Priest."

This amplified her doubts about being High Priestess and intensified her distress. She wasn't qualified. She lacked the training. She was just a teenager. *Who am I to think I can be High Priestess? Does anyone think I can?*

I do, came the words of the Sovereign, which materialized in Emma's head. *I say you're the High Priestess. That's all that matters. Pay these fringe fanatics no attention. Shove their words aside.*

Emma received the Sovereign's affirmation, pitting it against the assaulting words of her opposition: "Emma Barlow is not our High Priest."

You're wrong! Emma cried out in her spirit. *The Sovereign picked me. That's what matters.*

From then on, each time the protesters chanted "Emma Barlow is not our High Priest," she replaced their words with her own, as inspired by the Sovereign: "Emma Barlow *is* our High Priestess. Emma Barlow *is* our High Priestess. Emma Barlow *is* our High Priestess."

Emma breathed in. She breathed out. The peace that only the Sovereign could give flooded into her soul. It surged like a rushing tide that pushed away all that stood in its path. Everything was going to work out. She didn't know how, but it would.

Emma and Montgomery returned to her future office. Fred and Barney stood bent over her desk, looking at some large sheets of paper; they were architectural plans. Without saying a word, Emma edged up to the drawings. One sheet showed a large auditorium seating thousands, ten thousand she estimated. It was a clean, crisp design: practical, open, and inviting.

When Fred noticed Emma studying the drawing, he flipped the plans back to the opening page, a 3-D rendering of the completed structure. Emma gasped at the magnificent beauty of a building before her, a grand edifice reaching up into the sky.

"It's plans for a new auditorium," Barney explained. "I'd forgotten about them until we found them rolled up behind the filing cabinet. I authorized its development about fifteen years ago."

"It will seat 12,000," Fred explained. "The plan was to raze the old auditorium, Temple school, and dorms to make room for this. But we failed to secure funding. And, with declining attendance, there was no need for it. But now attendance is on the upswing."

"This makes it an opportune time to dust off these plans and move forward," Barney gushed. Emma had never seen him this excited about anything. But it figured that spending millions to build a huge shrine mattered to him. He might even view it as his legacy. "Not only will we need it soon, but it's now quite feasible." Barney tipped his head down as if to confirm the decision to move forward.

Emma shook her head. "As impressive as it is, building a huge auditorium we'll only use one hour a week isn't a good use of money. In fact, it's foolish. Instead, we should make the best use of what we do have and not waste funds on a new building. That's how we can best be good stewards of the Sovereign's money."

Barney sighed. "Will you at least consider it?"

Fred shook his head. "As exciting as a new building would be, Emma is correct. We must set such grandiose visions aside."

As the two men glared at each other, Chloe and Gabe returned. Both were grinning. Both had tear-streaked cheeks. And both their auras shone brightly in the spiritual realm.

"We are on our way to retrieve Barney's personal property from my quarters," Gabe said. Then he turned to Emma. "Would you deign to assist us in our quest?"

"Certainly," Emma said.

As they left, she whispered to them, "Given the restraining order, you two need to be careful about being seen together."

"We are quite safe here," Gabe said. "I trust the staff."

"What about Barney?" Emma asked.

"You raise a most astute concern," Gabe said. "I shall discuss the matter with him in private."

At that, their trio left and returned with three boxes. As they completed their second trip, Fred and Barney emerged from the office with boxes of their own. Completing their task, the office was now ready for Emma to use.

Chloe and Gabe left to spend the rest of the afternoon together. As they walked away, Chloe edged up to him and nudged his arm with her shoulder. Her hand reached out to hold his. He took it, and the two fell into step with each other as they strode out of view.

Fred left to talk to Lynn about the priests who had yet to return their ill-gained bonuses.

For once, Emma had nothing scheduled for the rest of the afternoon. "I'm going to try to talk with the protesters again," she said to Barney.

"Do you think that's wise?"

"I need to try," Emma said.

"I advise against it."

Emma glanced at Barney and lowered her eyebrows. His gaunt face suggested concern, but why would he be worried?

Emma headed toward the protesters, who now seemed louder than before. Montgomery followed.

After hesitating, Barney trudged behind them. But Emma didn't care if he went with her or not. In truth, she preferred he give her space.

As Emma rounded the corner and the protesters came into view, she realized why they sounded louder. Besides all ten priests, a dozen more civilians had joined them in their march and their chants.

She rolled her shoulders back, held her head high, and inhaled slowly. She asked the Sovereign for supernatural wisdom.

When she approached the edge of the group, she stopped and tried to make eye contact. Each one of them looked away. She asked if any of them wanted to talk. They all ignored her.

That's when she spotted three of the civilian protesters taking a break. They stood by a cluster of cars in the parking lot. Emma strolled up to them. They tensed as she approached.

"I'd like to hear what your concerns are," she said to the two women and one man.

The shorter woman spoke. "We have nothing against you, Emma," the woman said with a slight bow. "We accept you as our High Priestess. Our concern is what's happening in the Sunday services."

"I know that change is hard," Emma said. "That's why we're doing it slowly to give people time to understand."

"We feel our traditions slipping away—one by one," the woman said. "We want you to restore our old practices, not eliminate them. That's why we've joined the priests in their protest. The third part of their platform is the only one that concerns us."

Emma cocked her head to look at the woman. "Do you want our services to return to the way they were before I arrived?"

"Actually," the woman said, "we'd like to return to the way our services were twenty years ago, when we still met in the old auditorium."

"Tell me about it," Emma said. "What did you like?"

The woman relaxed her tense posture. She smiled for the first time. "We enjoyed our traditional hymns and hearing the majestic pipe organ. Especially the organ. We found comfort in the rhythm of our religious rituals. The choir sang for half the service, and the congregation didn't have to sing at all. That's what we grew up with, and that's what we want to experience again. But we see that disappearing completely under your leadership."

Emma glanced at the other two people. They

both nodded their confirmation. Emma paused. "I have an idea."

I like your idea, the Sovereign whispered to Emma's spirit.

"Let me show you something," Emma said. "Follow me."

She and Montgomery headed to the old auditorium. The three people followed her and beckoned their friends to join them. By the time they reached the auditorium, their group had swelled to fifteen. They entered through the main entrance to a bustle of activity from the cleaning crew.

Emma turned to face her entourage just as Barney trudged up. "The Sovereign told me to have this building cleaned up and ready to use again," Emma said. "I thought it might be for overflow seating on Sundays, but now I wonder if a better use might be to hold traditional services here and focus on reforming our practices at the new auditorium."

Emma didn't need to ask them what they thought. Their smiles, grins, and even tears confirmed they all liked her idea.

One man cleared his throat and timidly raised his hand. "What about the pipe organ? It's not been used in years. Does it even work anymore?"

"There's only one way to find out," came Barney's words from behind them. As everyone turned to stare, he marched toward the organ and sat on its bench. With practiced precision, his fingers fluttered over the controls, pushing buttons and flipping switches. He interlaced his fingers and rotated them away as he stretched out his arms. His knuckles cracked.

Now ready, his fingers hovered over the keys. He closed his eyes while inhaling slowly. Ready at last, he lowered his left hand. The tones of a glorious chord flowed from the pipes and reverberated through the space.

The protesters gasped in a reverent awe. All the workers stopped cleaning to watch. Barney lowered his right hand and launched into playing a traditional hymn. Though Emma didn't know it well, she recognized it as one of the people's most beloved songs.

The former protesters surged forward to encircle Barney as he played. The cleaning crew joined them. It was a holy moment. As the volume and the passion of Barney's playing increased, the space came alive as the music resounded off its walls.

When Barney played the hymn's concluding

notes, the people shouted. "Amen!" They applauded. Emma wasn't sure if they were praising the Sovereign's glory or Barney's playing. But the one thing she knew was that this was exactly what they wanted—and needed.

12

OPTIONS

Emma walked up to the group. Their excitement pleased her. Though her preferred form of worship was far from theirs, she now realized, for the first time, that not everyone approached the Sovereign—or practiced their faith—in the same way. Variety was good. Options were the answer.

"We think we'll have the cleaning done by the end of next week," she announced. "Perhaps we could have a practice service here a week from Sunday. Once we have all the kinks worked out, we can announce it and open it to everyone."

They responded as a group with pumped fists and a resounding "Yes!"

"I don't know what a traditional service was

like," Emma said. "Perhaps we can find a priest to head this up. If any of you are interested, you can meet with him and plan for a traditional service to be held here. How's that sound?"

Again, they all agreed.

Barney stood. "I suggest you tap Gavin. He'd be perfect for this role, and I think he'd relish it."

"Great idea," Emma said. "Will you text him?"

"I'd be most honored to," came a voice from within the crowd.

Emma turned to her right. There stood Gavin. He beamed and waved a glove-covered hand. He stepped forward as he wiped his sweaty forehead with the sleeve of his shirt. Then he removed his latex gloves and shoved them into his pocket. "If you want, we can meet in five minutes, just as soon as I clean up a bit."

"Who wants to provide input for our new traditional services?" Emma asked.

Fifteen hands shot up. Every one of the civilian protesters wanted to take part. From now on, they'd be part of the solution and not part of the problem.

As Gavin hustled off, everyone turned back to Emma. "Besides planning the contents of the service, we'll need to find people to take part and help lead it. Since you want a choir, they'll need time to practice. We also need to figure out what time you want the service to start and how long it will last."

Barney's fingers, that had just dazzled them with his playing, now danced over his phone as he entered Emma's list. "With your permission, High Priestess, I'll relay this information to Gavin and assist him for the remainder of my shift."

Though this would violate Barney's mandate to always be at Emma's side, they'd already strayed from it once today, so she reasoned another deviation wouldn't hurt.

The cleaning crew returned to their labor with renewed enthusiasm. They now had a tangible goal to work toward and not a task with a vague intent.

The fifteen former protesters turned inward in excitement. They all started talking at once.

Barney ambled up to Emma. "Thank you for allowing me to take part in this. I appreciate your confidence."

"I'm still shocked at your stirring performance," Emma said. "I didn't know you could play."

"There's much about me you don't know, High Priestess." Barney gave her the slightest of bows.

I wonder what he means. Should I be worried?

13

CLEARING CONFUSION

Though Emma wanted to take part in the discussion, she needed to give Gavin the space to handle his assignment. This was the purpose of delegation, a skill she still struggled with.

When Gavin returned, Emma raised both arms and proclaimed a blessing on the group. "May the Sovereign guide your thoughts and anoint your words as you plan for the service. May you be filled with peace and experience joy in your discussions. Amen."

As Gavin led his group to a meeting room, Emma left to find Joshua. It didn't take her long. She spotted him well before he spotted her. With the bounce in his step and a grin on his face, he strode down the path.

At last, Joshua looked up and saw Emma. He stopped walking and stared. "Wow. You're hot!" His face turned a light shade of pink and he squirmed. "What I mean is you look more beautiful than ever."

"Nice recovery." Emma smirked. "Apology accepted." She thanked him with a smile and a wink. "Compliment received."

"Seriously, you're beautiful."

"Had my hair trimmed this afternoon."

Joshua snapped his fingers. "That's it! Your hair. It frames your face and shimmies when you walk."

"Aside from being enthralled by my beauty, you seem quite pleased about something else. Spill."

"Got my first Temple paycheck today." Joshua beamed. "Having a job and earning money feels like my first step to becoming an adult."

Emma scratched her cheek. "Temple paycheck?"

"For sure. Chloe got hers too. The rest of your disciples will get their first one next time." That's when Joshua noticed the confusion on Emma's face. "Didn't you get yours?"

"I'm here to serve the Sovereign. I have everything I need: food and a place to stay," Emma said. "Until today, I never thought about money."

"Still, you need to get paid. What about when you want new clothes? Or decide to buy a car?"

"I'll need my driver's license first."

"Me too," Joshua said. "But I'm saving for a car . . . and for when we get married."

"Yeah, there's that too. But we've got time. Lots of it."

"I'm sure them not paying you is an oversight. Let's find Frederick and get it straightened out."

The pair pivoted to Emma's left and strode to the palace where Fred's office was. Emma rapped on the door frame as she walked in. She opened her mouth to speak, but for once she wasn't sure what to say. She didn't want to come across as greedy, accusatory, or demanding. But not being paid— when everyone else was—irked her.

Joshua came to her rescue. "Frederick, there's a problem with Emma's pay. What do we need to do to fix it?"

Fred looked up as a pleased smile formed on his face. He gestured for them to sit. Leaning back, he crossed his arms. "There's no problem. We've been paying Emma all along. It's just that she doesn't know it."

"Now I'm really confused," Emma said.

Fred leaned forward. "We wanted to pay you from the very beginning, but your father knew you'd never accept it. So your mother set up a bank account for you, and Topher's been depositing your paycheck there ever since."

"It's nice to have people watching out for me." Emma cocked her head to the side as she formed her question. "Just curious. How much am I making?"

"Like all priests, you receive minimum wage. In your case it's converted to a salary, just as with me and other department heads and leaders. Topher's working on increasing that soon. And not that you likely care, but you also have a pension and health-care insurance."

"Thanks," Emma said. "I never thought about having money until today when I wanted to tip Ashley."

"I'm glad you didn't," Fred said. "Temple staff are prohibited from accepting tips."

"Good to know." Emma began to stand, but Fred signaled for her to remain. "If I may, I have a query for you. It's been gnawing at me for a while."

With a nod, Emma encouraged Fred to continue.

"When you divided the priests into groups, you put me in my own: Delta Group. But you never added any priests to the group or told me what I'm supposed to do. In this regard, I feel forgotten."

Emma looked at the floor. She'd made an error and now she needed to own it. "I'm sorry. That was my mistake."

"It's not a problem," Fred said. "But I'd like to know your expectations."

Emma looked up and gazed steadily at Fred. "I blew it. The Sovereign told me to put the priests into three groups. But I got carried away and made a fourth group just for you. But that wasn't what the Sovereign wanted."

"How do we fix it?" Fred asked.

"Let's forget about Delta Group. You've been functioning in Gamma Group, and that's where you should be. But I do have a special assignment for you." Emma felt tension leave her body as she worked to correct her mistake. "I'd like you to look for priests—or staff, for that matter—who can become leaders. You have good insight into people, and I need your guidance."

"I already have some people in mind."

"I'm sure you do," Emma said.

"Any position in particular?"

Emma shook her head, but she was lying. How could she tell her most trusted ally to look for a replacement for himself? Why had the Sovereign told her to prepare for him to leave?

14

PRIESTS AND PROBLEMS

As they left the palace, Emma thanked Joshua for helping her talk with Fred about her paycheck. "Are you really saving money for us to get married?"

"A car first," Joshua clarified. "A wedding second."

"At least I know where I stand." Emma flashed him a crooked grin.

As they neared the parking lot where Joshua's mother would pick him up, Chloe and Gabe strolled up. "Forget you saw that," Emma hissed to Joshua. "Their relationship is top secret. No one can know. Especially Chloe's dad."

At the sight of them, Gabe spun around and hustled away, moving faster than Emma had ever seen him move. A worried Chloe approached Joshua. "Don't tell anyone you saw us together. Please. Promise me."

Joshua held up his right hand. "Promise. Do you want me to pinky swear too?"

"I'm serious," Chloe said.

"I am too," Joshua answered. "Your secret is safe with me."

Emma gave Joshua a goodbye hug and then turned to Chloe. Leaning in to embrace her best friend, Emma whispered in her ear. "I'm so excited for you and Gabe. Let me know if you need anything."

That's when Joshua's mom arrived. Joshua climbed in the front seat, and Chloe got in the back.

Emma waved goodbye to her friends. As they drove away, she headed to the cafeteria for supper with the priests. When Emma walked up, Gavin was already gushing about plans to start a traditional service in the old auditorium. He bubbled with excitement. The other priests fed off his enthusiasm. Three of them offered to help.

Emma sat next to Ezra, who was heading up his own plans for the ancient Temple. "He's given me an interesting idea," he whispered to Emma.

"When you're ready to share, please tell me," she whispered back.

During a lull in the group's conversation, Mark turned to Emma. "Though our conclusions are not indefensible, we concur that nothing in the Holy Text prohibits women from being priests. Any restrictions address specific situations, which no longer apply. Having only men serve seems more cultural than scriptural."

"Good to know," Emma said. "Are you open to research another topic?"

Mark gleamed. "Most certainly."

"I can think of two wedding ceremonies recorded in the Holy Text," Emma said. "There was Mateo marrying Yael and Noam marrying Avigail. Any other mentions of ancient weddings? Again, not urgent. Whenever you have time."

"We'll start on it tomorrow morning," Mark confirmed. "I'm curious why you're interested."

"As High Priestess I can conduct weddings, but I don't have a clue what to do. As a starting point, I'd like to know what the Holy Text says."

"I sense we may see a reform in our wedding ceremonies too." Mark's eyes twinkled. "I'll be most interested to see what you come up with."

As the priests' discussion turned to other things,

Emma's mind retreated inward. She wondered what Ezra was thinking about. Not knowing excited her almost as much as knowing. She also wondered how she might conduct Ashley and Topher's wedding. At least she had a couple of months to think about it.

One by one, the priests said good night and headed to their rooms.

When only Emma and Fred remained, he moved to sit next to her. "A couple of quick updates: First, three of the priests in Alpha group want to meet with us tomorrow about returning their unethical bonuses. We're meeting with Lynn at two. Please join us."

"Will do!"

"Second, Elizabeth will join us next week, and you can offer a job to Hernandez."

"Elizabeth? Who's that?"

"Elizabeth Butler. Your former religion teacher. You offered her a job last week, remember?"

Emma perked up. "Got it! I never knew her first name."

"Last, as we suspected, Barney paid off the guards to not implicate him in the threats and attacks on you. This ensures he'll avoid prosecution."

"Let me guess," Emma ventured, "a million each?"

"Correct."

Emma groaned. "First, he paid off the four women and now the guards. That's strike two for us."

"Our third and final chance to put him away is his misuse of Temple funds to give unauthorized bonuses," Fred said. "I understand they plan to arrest him and the other priests next week. They'll charge him with misappropriation of funds, embezzlement, and conspiracy to commit fraud."

"I hope that sticks," Emma said. "Will we get the money back?"

Fred shook his head. "Doubtful."

15

FRIENDSHIP BRACELET

Emma trudged to her room. She knew she should be grateful for the chance to recover the improper bonus money from three more priests. But all she could think about was the other seven and especially all the money Barney had siphoned off for himself.

Though they didn't have an exact number, a conservative estimate was that it was enough to fund all their capital improvement projects and then some. Plus they could also make a nice emergency fund.

This preoccupied her as she got ready for bed.

At last Emma was ready to study the Holy Text. Only she wasn't. She lacked focus. The Sovereign deserved better. Emma closed her eyes and breathed in. She breathed out. She inhaled peace and exhaled distraction. "Lord," she prayed aloud, "sharpen my attention as I study Scripture tonight. Open my soul to receive the insight that only you can provide."

Emma placed her copy of the Holy Text on her desk, sat her journal to its right, and lit the candles on either side. She turned off the light and sat in her broken-down chair, which offered little back support and provided much discomfort. Yet the physical ache it produced sharpened her spiritual comprehension.

But she still wasn't ready. She must complete her ritual first—silly as it was.

She tipped her head down to rest her forehead on the leather cover of the sacred Text. Remaining in that reverent position, she counted to thirty. She sat up and strained her arms heavenward. "Guide my study, oh Sovereign Lord."

Emma held that position for about ten seconds, though this time she didn't count. She relaxed her posture and concluded her prayer. "May it be so."

At last, Emma was fully ready—body, soul, and spirit—to immerse herself in the precious words of the Holy Text. She turned to the next passage for her to explore, the section marked by the maroon ribbon: Prophecy 102.

Emma read. Emma studied. And Emma meditated on the sacred words of the Holy Text. When bursts of inspiration came, she made furious notes in her journal. One page. Two pages. And then a third. It seemed she'd only just begun when she checked the time. It was ten o'clock, her bedtime at home, even though she no longer had to follow her parents' rules.

With a sigh, Emma closed the text and her notebook. She blew out the two candles. As she spun to take the two steps to her bed, the Sovereign stopped her. *Check Chloe's friendship bracelet.*

Emma didn't want to. More than anything, she wanted to climb into bed and sleep. Yet obedience was more important. In the dark, she shuffled to the door and fumbled for the light switch. With its mechanical click, light from the room's single bulb filled the place. She blinked as she adjusted to the sudden illumination.

Emma glanced at her left wrist that proudly bore Chloe's friendship bracelet. They had exchanged these gifts at the end of middle school with a pledge to be BFFs. Though Chloe's bracelet broke that summer, Emma protected hers as the cherished gift it was. Well-worn and much loved, wearing the bracelet filled Emma with joy.

Looks fine to me, she said to the Sovereign.

Look closer, came the Sovereign's reply.

Emma rotated her wrist to look at the friendship bracelet from different angles. Everything looked okay. Then she spun it around to see the other side. Wait. Something looked off. What was it? A new bead? How could that be?

Emma brought her wrist closer and squinted at the bracelet. Though the light had seemed bright when she first turned it on, her eyes couldn't make out what she wanted to see. Emma grabbed her phone and turned on its light, directing the beam at her wrist.

She gasped.

Connected to her bracelet was an electronic device, just like the one on Hernandez's coat collar. It was a bug. How long had Barney been listening in on her conversations?

How did he ever plant a bug on her friendship bracelet without her knowing it? Yet he had somehow managed. How long had it been there? How much did he know? Certainly, he heard what Fred had told her that evening. This meant Barney knew he faced arrest next week.

Though Emma had never taken Chloe's friendship bracelet off the entire time she had had it, that's exactly what she needed to do now. As her fingers fumbled and twisted and tugged, eventually the knotted fastener gave way.

Now, what should she do?

Sound waves. Hernandez had said the device picked up sound waves. Emma needed to block sound. She laid the bracelet on her desk and retrieved the plastic cup from her bathroom. Turning the cup over, she placed it over the bracelet. Not satisfied, she wrapped a hand towel around the cup to further dampen audio. Then she set a book on top of everything to hold it in place.

She turned off the light and slid into bed. But thoughts about what to do with the bug assaulted her mind. Sleep eluded her.

16

PROTESTS EBB AND FLOW

Emma awoke in the morning, not rested and still concerned. Aside from having Barney invade her privacy by listening to her conversations, it felt wrong not having Chloe's friendship bracelet adorn her wrist. It would take some getting used to. Emma hurriedly showered, fighting her panic at being in such a tight space even more than usual.

She dressed, ate breakfast with the priests, and hustled off to school, relieved to be putting some distance between herself and Barney's bug back in her room.

As she neared school, the sound of the priests' protest reached her ears before the sight of their activity. Their chants had changed. "Restore our traditions. Banish all heresy."

When Emma rounded the corner of the walkway, the protesters came into view. This morning, there were only seven priests and no civilians. The strength of their protest was waning, yet their words assaulted Emma just as before.

"Restore our traditions. Banish all heresy."

Emma attempted to talk with them. They just chanted louder.

"Restore our traditions. Banish all heresy."

Emma gritted her teeth, dashed into the building, and scooted to class. She plopped down between Joshua and Chloe.

Chloe noticed Emma's bare wrist right away and cast a concerned glance at Emma. "What happened to our friendship bracelet?"

"Something came up, and I couldn't wear it today. But no worries, we're still BFFs."

"You know no one says that anymore, don't you?"

"When have I ever cared what people think? Whatever you call it, we're still besties. Always will be."

Emma pivoted to peek at Barney. He sat in his

usual spot in the back corner of the room. His copy of the Holy Text sat before him, unopened. Instead, he worked furiously on his phone.

Emma sent Lane a quick text, asking for him to meet her after lunch. Then she turned off her phone and began her schoolwork. Periodically, she would check on Barney. Each time she glanced his way, he was busy texting.

What's he up to?

The bracelet didn't come up again until school was over at noon, but it wasn't Chloe who mentioned it.

"Why aren't you wearing Chloe's friendship bracelet?" Barney asked Emma as they exited the classroom. "Did you two have a fight?"

Emma had a ready answer. "It was bugging me. I took it off."

Barney blinked once but said nothing.

Emma wasn't sure if his blink was coincidence or a surprise reaction that snuck out before he could mask it. She bent down and ruffled Montgomery's head before petting his back. He received her attention with a vigorous headshake and an enthusiastic tail wag.

Finished, Emma stood and strode toward the

front of the building. She wanted to check on the protesters. But what she saw was not what she expected. Joining the seven priests were more civilians. Perhaps twenty. Maybe more.

Spotting four of them taking a break in the parking lot, she strolled up to them. "Can we talk?"

They shook their heads. "Sorry, High Priestess," one of them whispered, "they warned us not to talk to you." All four turned their backs to her.

Emma groaned, hopefully to herself. The protest was flowing again, even surging. This battle was far from over.

The discouraged High Priestess shrugged and headed to the cafeteria. She met with her team as usual for their working lunch. With all the updates done, but before they finished eating, Emma excused herself. But instead of ducking into the restroom, she ditched Barney. It felt so good.

Lane waited for her at the lower-level entrance to the priests' quarters.

"Thanks for your help," Emma said. "I don't have any tools to take care of it myself."

"No problem."

Emma walked up to the door and opened it for

Lane. She gestured for him to go inside. "My room is the first door on the right. The bracelet is on my desk underneath the book."

"Aren't you coming?"

"Wouldn't be proper."

"Don't you trust me?"

"It's other people I worry about," Emma said.

"I never thought you cared what other people think."

"Gabe tells me that as High Priestess, I need to avoid even the hint of impropriety. It's the Sovereign's reputation at stake. I do care about that."

"Impropriety?"

"You know, anything that could look wrong."

Lane shrugged. "Whatever." He shuffled inside while Emma waited outside. In thirty seconds he was back. "Here's your bracelet, good as new. Well, not quite new, but certainly bug free." He held up a plastic vial with the offending gadget securely inside. He shook it with vigor. "That will certainly give someone an earful."

Emma left the grinning Lane, shaking the vial once again. She headed to her office in the palace. It felt so good to say *her* office.

She sat in her chair, leaned back, and crossed her arms. She couldn't help but smile.

Then Fred walked in and interrupted her glee. "I thought you might be here. That's good. We need to talk before our meeting with the priests at two."

17

A TINY WRINKLE

With her hands clenched, Emma stomped into the conference room and plopped onto the center chair. She landed with a thud. Words of Fred's recent confession echoed in her head, and she suppressed the tears that threatened to gush forth. She forced out a deep sigh, still struggling to process what she had learned.

The bonus-money meeting with the priests wouldn't start for another fifteen minutes. She'd need at least that much time to calm her rage. *Fill me with your peace*, she prayed silently. *Show me how to respond to what Fred did and how to make things right with Barney.*

Lane can help, came the Sovereign's succinct reply.

Emma relaxed as she took in the Sovereign's peace. She pulled out her phone and sent Lane a lengthy text. Then she sent Barney a much shorter one. *Don't know where you are but meet me in my office at three.*

Content she was addressing the second half of the problem, she still needed to figure out what to do with Fred. But that would have to wait.

The three priests filed into the room, greeting Emma with an encouraging nod. Relaxed and smiling, they sat across from her. Fred and Lynn arrived soon after, with Topher trailing behind. Mark, as Chief of Priests, joined them right at two. He sat next to the three repentant priests.

As before, Lynn patiently reviewed the agreement, explaining each clause and answering questions along the way. Emma had heard it all before, but one additional clause surprised her. The section said that as part of the agreement, the priests' employment at the Temple would immediately end.

Why did the first group receive mercy and the second group receive judgment? Emma wondered.

It took Lynn most of the hour to explain the entire document. When she finished, she laid her copy on the table and looked at the three priests with an inviting smile. "Who would like to sign first?"

The priests looked at each other, shaking their heads. The one in the center spoke. "We've decided not to sign."

Mark reacted immediately. "Why not? Yesterday you said you were more than ready to put this behind you."

"The first group got to keep their jobs, but we don't," the priest answered. "We want the same deal they got, or we won't sign."

"The first priests returned all of their improper bonus money," Fred explained. "But you can't because you've spent some of it or lost it in bad investments. Since you're only making partial restitution, we feel it unwise to allow your continued employment here."

Emma looked at the priests' spirits. For the first time since she'd met them, each one had a hint of color, replacing their normal blackness. Something in their souls was changing, slowly to be sure; spiritually they were now moving in the right direction.

Emma leaned forward. "Why do you want to keep working here?"

"We know we opposed everything you've done

since you arrived," their spokesman said. "But we want to make amends. Returning as much of the money as we can is the first step. The next step is making a positive difference here at the Temple."

"I'd like to see you have the chance," Emma said. Still angry with Fred, she didn't want to confer with him, even though she knew she should. Instead, she turned to Lynn. "Will you remove that one section?"

The accommodating attorney nodded. Taking the closest priest's contract, she put a big X through the offending clause and drew a line next to it for the priest to initial. She repeated that with the other two contracts. All three priests signed immediately, beaming as they did.

Topher opened his laptop, which they would use to transfer the funds. He turned it toward the priests and walked around the table. "Who wants to go first?"

All three signaled with their hands and said, "I do."

18

MORE SURVEILLANCE

Emma ignored Fred as she left the conference room. She stomped straight to her office but paused when she reached the doorway. Not only was Barney there, but he was sitting at the desk—her desk.

Emma glared at him. "That's my chair."

Barney shrugged. "Old habits." A hint of his former arrogance played on his face.

Montgomery sat on Barney's lap, content with all the attention he was receiving from his usually distant owner.

Choosing to not confront Barney about his seating selection, Emma sat across from him. Montgomery perked up at Emma's presence, leapt from his master's lap, trotted across the desk, and jumped onto Emma's lap. He burrowed down. As soon as Emma stroked his head, he rested his chin on her thigh and closed his eyes. He let out a happy puppy sigh.

Barney scowled at his dog.

When Lane arrived, he sat in the remaining chair, which also faced Barney. Placing his laptop on the desk, he opened it and began typing.

"What's the meaning of this?" Barney demanded.

Asking for the Sovereign's guidance, Emma chose her words with care. "A mistake was made, and we want to fix it. Please give Lane your phone."

"I will not," Barney said. "It contains personal information, and I desire to keep that private."

"We provided the phone for your work here at the Temple. We own it, and we pay for it." With an open hand, Emma curled her fingers toward her, beckoning him to comply.

After a brief stare down, he handed Emma his phone. She started to pass it to Lane, but he stopped her. "Though it's not necessary," Lane said, "it will go much quicker if I don't have to hack the login."

Barney retrieved the phone from Emma, signed

in, and handed the device to Lane. Lane connected it to his laptop.

"I deserve an explanation," Barney said. "My patience is growing thin."

"I learned this afternoon," Emma said, "that surveillance software was installed on your phone. That was wrong, and I apologize. It's been logging all your communications, tracking everywhere you went, and listening to everything you said."

"This is completely unacceptable." Barney pounded his fist on the table, jarring Montgomery from his sleep, who jerked his head up before settling back down. "You've invaded my privacy."

"It stings to have someone listening in on your conversations without your knowledge, doesn't it?" Emma retorted.

Barney opened his mouth but hesitated. Instead, he relaxed his frame. "Point made. I apologize for my outrage."

"Lane is removing that software," Emma added.

"Did he install it?"

"Certainly not," Emma said.

Barney paused for a few seconds and then perked up. "It was Junior! That infuriating ingrate Junior added spyware to my phone without my

knowledge. I demand you terminate him immediately."

"First, his name is Frederick," Emma corrected,
"not Junior. Please use his real name. Second, it
isn't your phone—remember? Third, the person
who did this will be punished, but that's not your
concern. Last, you're in enough trouble on your
own."

"I've done nothing but faithfully serve you ever
since my reinstatement," Barney said. "If nothing
else, you should commend me."

Emma gave him a sad smile as she shook her
head. "We now know you've been working behind
my back this whole time. You've encouraged the
priests to not return their bonus money. You've
agitated a rebellion against me. And you're the one
behind the civilians who continue to join the
protest. Also, you've been colluding with the Prime
Minister to seize control of the Temple and the
state. If anyone should be terminated, it should be
you."

"You obtained this information illegally,"
Barney sputtered. "It will never stand up in court."

"It doesn't have to," Emma said, "because we'll
never use it. In fact, I ordered the information be

deleted. And Lane is making sure no new data will ever be collected."

"This is sophisticated software," Lane said. "Although using it was wrong, I admire the creativity of the code."

"It's beyond me how Junior—I mean, Frederick—could pull off such a sophisticated feat." Barney shook his head.

"Didn't you know," Emma said, "that before he became a priest, he was head of software development at a hi-tech company?"

Barney shook his head. "I'll never underestimate him again."

Lane unplugged the phone from his laptop and handed it back to Barney. "I've removed the rogue software and returned your phone to normal use."

"Are you sure?"

"The only way to be 100 percent sure," Lane said, "is to wipe the phone and start fresh."

"Or I could just purchase a new one," Barney said.

"Yeah," Lane answered, "there's that too."

Barney stood. "Permit me to take the rest of the afternoon to process this unfortunate development. I must consult with my attorney to consider our options." Barney headed toward the door and stopped to glare at his dog. He snapped his fingers. "Come, Montgomery. We must depart."

19

RESTORING TRADITIONS

After Barney and his pooch left, Lane looked at Emma. "What are you going to do with Frederick?"

"Not sure. Still waiting for direction from the Sovereign, but for now I want to check with Gavin on his progress at the old auditorium. Care to go with?"

"I'm headed there too," Lane said.

"Does that mean you're done with the communication backlog?"

Lane shook his head. "Far from it. We're caught up on texts and voicemail, but we still have a way to go on email. And it will take weeks to wade through the bags of snail mail."

"Then shouldn't you go to the communications office instead?"

"We're all temporarily reassigned to clean the old auditorium. They're trying to get it ready for this Sunday."

"We don't need it until next Sunday," Emma clarified. When Lane didn't respond, she changed the subject. "What do you see yourself doing after you graduate from school? A tech industry career?"

"I want to become a priest," Lane said. "We all do. That's why we're here. Even the girls, though it's an iffy choice for them."

"What do you mean, all?" Emma asked.

"All twelve of us, of course. All your disciples. We knew there was something special about you. That's why we followed you. We wanted to be part of it. Now we can."

Emma considered his words. "Did you know I was going to become High Priestess?"

"We didn't—not at all. But none of us were surprised either. You seem destined for it."

"It was a shock for me, that's for sure," Emma said. "But if I can be High Priestess, then the girls in our group can certainly become priests. There's nothing specific in the Holy Text that says priests must be male. It's a cultural thing, not scriptural."

The discussion ended when they entered the old auditorium to a flurry of cleaning. Lane returned to his assignment while Emma strolled up to Gavin.

His face lit up when he saw her. "I'm so glad you're here. I have exciting updates."

"That's why I came," Emma said. "What you're doing here is important."

Gavin brimmed with excitement. "Our group has put together a splendid plan for the service. We're striving to be ready to launch on Sunday."

"Maybe this Sunday should be a trial run," Emma suggested, "to be ready for next week."

"We have much interest and growing momentum," Gavin countered. "I feel the Sovereign's prompting for us to have our practice service tomorrow. Then we can be ready for a real service on Sunday. We have nearly fifty people interested."

"I may be able to point you to some more."

Gavin raised his eyebrows.

"There's another group of protesters who joined the priests today." Emma explained. "They won't talk to me, but I suspect if you show up around five as they're winding down for the day, they might talk to you."

"How many?"

"Didn't count. Maybe two dozen. But it wouldn't surprise me if more showed up."

A gleam formed on Gavin's face. "I wonder if they'd be interested in doing some cleaning. The protesters from Thursday are all here today." Gavin gestured to the people busily at work.

Emma recognized some of them. Their commitment to Gavin's vision thrilled her. "Just wait for the priests to leave before you approach this new group," Emma advised. "Maybe they'll be more interested in worshiping with you on Sunday than protesting."

Emma took a few steps away from Gavin but then spun around. "Wait! We have a conflict."

Gavin's eyes popped open. "What?"

"It's the choir. They can't be in two places at once. They're already committed to singing for the service in the other auditorium this Sunday."

The concern on Gavin's face melted away. "You must be unaware that we have two choirs. They perform on alternate Sundays, so they don't burn out. For the short term, however, they're willing to forgo their off Sundays to make sure we have a choir in both auditoriums."

"It seems you have it all figured out," Emma said. "Sorry I interfered."

"It's not a problem. I appreciate input from as many sources as possible. Especially yours."

Emma said goodbye to Gavin and took a deep breath. "Thank you, everyone," she projected from her diaphragm, "for all your hard work in getting everything ready for Sunday." She waved goodbye and then left.

She had one more stop, the ancient Temple. But then she wouldn't be able to procrastinate any longer. She'd have to have a hard conversation with Fred. Emma shoved that to the back of her mind— for now.

Striding with purpose, Emma walked up to the ancient Temple. Priests and people milled about. One priest addressed a group of tourists, telling them about ancient worship practices. Another priest explained the building's architecture to his group. And still another gave a tour inside the structure.

Ezra was there too. She waited for him to finish with his group. When he saw her, he ran up and gave her a hug. Then he pulled away. "I hope that wasn't inappropriate."

"I don't think anyone can get too many hugs," Emma said.

"I'm so glad you stopped by so you can see what

we're doing. The number of visitors we receive each day has tripled since you arrived."

"This is my first daytime visit to the ancient Temple since I've become High Priestess. I've wanted to come back, but there never seems to be enough time."

"We interact with each guest, regardless of why they came," Ezra explained. "Some are tourists, others are pilgrims, and a few are just curious. Our goal is to make a difference in the life of everyone who visits."

"Making a difference should be the goal of everyone here," Emma said. "I'm glad to see you leading the way."

"It's the most meaningful thing I've done during my entire time here," Ezra said. "Thank you for allowing me to pursue my passion. The other priests here feel the same way. We desire to shine a light on our faith's past."

"About that," Emma said. "I just checked in with Gavin at the old auditorium. They're preparing to launch a traditional service there this Sunday and not next. So exciting. No pressure and no rush, but I wonder what you'd think about one day holding an ancient service here?"

"I'm so glad you asked," Ezra said. "Last night's

discussion sparked that very idea, and I can't stop thinking about it. But we have much to do first. As they say, walk before you run."

"If there's anything I can do to help, just ask," Emma said. "This is important to me."

20

ANSWERED PRAYER

Emma left the ancient Temple, excited for Ezra, what he was doing there, and his vision for the future. Yet the situation with Fred weighed on her being—heavily. He was wrong to have installed spyware on Barney's phone. It was probably illegal too. Should she offer him mercy or demand justice?

Was this why the Sovereign had told her to be prepared to replace Fred? Until this incident, he'd been such a valued ally, a most trusted resource. She didn't want to fire him.

She was glad Barney had left after Lane removed the spyware. Her aide's constant presence grated on her, and it was nice not to have him hovering, to not have to worry about what she said.

Even though she had fantasized many times about firing Barney, Emma had never fired anyone.

Yet at this moment, Barney wasn't her concern. Fred was. She paused to pray about what to do— again.

I'm confused, Emma prayed in her mind. *You've prepared me to say goodbye to Fred, but I thought it would be way in the future. I didn't think I'd have to fire him. I don't want to, but that seems to be what I must do. If you have a different plan, just let me know—soon.*

Emma had stopped walking while she prayed. She had even closed her eyes. When she looked up, Fred walked her way. Though Fred never moved fast, his gait seemed even slower today. It was almost like a waddle.

As he moved closer, she noticed the normal sparkle from his eyes was gone. He clamped his lips together. His pale face contrasted to his normal glow. He didn't seem so huggable anymore.

Emma waited for Fred to reach her. Should she just say "you're fired" and be done with it? Or should she explain why? Was it appropriate for her to add an "I'm sorry" to the end? What if he cried? What if *she* cried?

Her pulse raced faster with each of his approaching steps. Her heart thumped in her chest, as if it were about to explode. Maybe it was. She rehearsed the words in her mind. *I'm sorry, Fred, but I have to let you go.*

That was it. Don't say *fired*. Say *let you go*. That would be softer.

Should she have security present in case he didn't react well? But it was too late for that. What about his keys? His passwords? All the critical knowledge in his head?

He was now only ten feet away. Emma slowly sucked in a lungful of air—and resolve.

Now he was only five feet in front of her. She braced herself for what would happen. He took two more steps toward her and stopped. She opened her mouth, but before she could say a thing, he held up his hand.

"I know you have every reason to fire me," Fred said. "That's what I would do. But please let me say my piece first. I want to tell you how sorry I am for what I did. Installing spyware on Barney's phone was wrong and illegal. It doesn't matter that I did so only to keep you safe. I deserve whatever punishment awaits me. I will accept it and won't fight it.

"Though I can't find Barney to tell him how sorry I am, I did text him. I'll apologize in person the first chance I get—assuming I get one. I know I deserve judgment for what I did. But I ask you to consider offering me mercy instead. As we read in the Holy Text, the Sovereign did that for Yonatan when he stole from the people's offerings and used it to buy a field.

"I know I've lost your trust. I'll need to earn it back—providing you allow me the chance. If you do, know that I will do my utmost to make sure you never have to question my integrity or my loyalty again."

Fred looked like he wanted to say more, but he huffed to catch his breath.

This time it was Emma who held up her hand. She now knew exactly what to tell him. The Sovereign had just given her the exact words to say.

"Fred, I forgive you."

21

SUNDAY SURPRISE

Sunday morning, Emma waited in her dressing room behind the stage in the auditorium. She was ready for the service. Well, almost ready. She wore her light tan priestly robe. She and Mark had prayed for the service, and she was going over what she planned to share about Talia, the young girl who led the army to victory when none of the men would.

Emma closed her eyes to focus her spirit on the service as she waited for Ashley to do her makeup, which was usually no more than a light powder dusting on her forehead to reduce camera glare.

Sovereign Lord, she prayed silently, *bless our service and guide me in my part of it today. May you be honored with the results, and may it advance your kingdom. So be it.*

"Sorry I'm late, my Emma."

Emma's eyes popped open at the sound of her friend's voice. There stood a harried Ashley.

"Mark took longer than usual," Ashley explained, "but I see you're almost ready. It'll only take a sec."

Ashley opened her oversized cosmetics case on the table. She pulled out a fluffy powder brush and some powder. "Did you hear about the protesters out front?"

"How many are there today?" Emma asked.

"I guess forty or fifty, but you know numbers aren't my thing, so I may be way off."

Emma sighed. "Even one is too many. Next Sunday we'll have a solution. So for today, I'll try not to think about them."

After a burst of brushing, Ashley stepped back to survey Emma. "You look great. You're ready for the service." The cosmetologist placed the brush and powder back in her case and clicked it shut. She lugged it to the door. But she didn't leave. Instead, she stopped and spun around. "This seems a little weird, but I think I'm supposed to pray for you. Is that okay?"

Emma stood and walked toward the hesitant

young woman. "I always appreciate it when people pray for me."

Ashley hesitated. "Am I supposed to hold up my hands or something?"

"Whatever you're comfortable with. The Sovereign cares more about what's in our heart when we pray than how we do it."

"Okay then. Let's do this. Sovereign, please bless Emma during our service. May she hear from you and do what you say. Aah, okay then. I guess that's it. Aah, thank you, Lord. I mean, Amen."

"That was a wonderful prayer." Then Emma held up her hand toward Ashley. "And bless Ashley's time this afternoon with Topher. May their relationship honor you. Amen."

Twenty minutes later, Emma was still thinking about Ashley and her prayer as she waited on stage for her cue. Her friend's heartfelt prayer touched her. The young woman's faith was growing. That excited Emma.

Emma had already welcomed the people to the service. Mark had gone through the first set of rituals, as proclaimed in the Holy Text. Now it was Emma's turn to give today's lesson. She stood and walked toward the dais.

"Today I want to share with you the story about

Talia. I'd planned it for last week, but I was off helping to free the prisoners. Talia's story starts in History 117.1.

"Talia was the youngest in her family and the least esteemed. She was a shepherdess in charge of watching over her family's sheep. One day when she was by herself in the field tending to her flock, the Sovereign spoke to her. Talia heard audible words. The Sovereign said, 'Follow me.' That was it. And that's exactly what Talia did.

"The Sovereign spoke, and Talia obeyed . . ." Emma squirmed a bit. "Talia abandoned her sheep . . . and trusted that the Sovereign's call was more important than . . ." Emma shifted from one foot to the other, "more important than doing what seemed to be the responsible thing."

Emma glanced up as she considered what she was about to do. It felt both wrong and right at the same time. Pushing back the hair from the front of her face, she scrutinized the audience. "I'm so sorry to do this, but I need to leave. Right now. The Sovereign just told me to take care of something. Um, maybe the choir can sing while I'm gone."

She stepped aside from the dais, fumbled to turn off her mic, and walked boldly forward, jumping off the stage. The people gasped. She had done it once before, only this time she knew what to expect. When her feet hit the floor, she dashed forward down the main aisle toward the exit. The people watched her in shock. By the time she hit the panic bar on the door, music had started, and the choir's singing wafted forth.

22

BAD BARNEY/GOOD BARNEY

Protesters marched outside, their chants and their signs aligned with a call for Emma to return to holding traditional services. There were at least fifty people. A grinning Barney stood at the peripheral of the group's protest.

Emma rushed up to him. "When I gave you permission to be here on Sunday morning, it was to attend the service, not organize a protest."

Barney's smile faded, and he glanced away. When he turned his attention back to Emma, a repentant look replaced his former arrogance. "I'm so sorry, Emma, for disappointing you again. It seems I don't do what I want to do and keep doing what I don't want to do. I am a man in profound misery."

"We'll talk about this more on Monday, but right now I must deal with this." She turned her attention to the protesters and called out, "I have good news."

They ceased chanting and stopped marching.

"We've heard your concerns and are working to address them." Emma projected as loudly as she could without yelling. "If you want to come with me, I'll show you."

Emma walked a couple of steps away. The people lowered their signs but seemed hesitant to follow her. "You can keep complaining, or you can come with me to see what we're working on. Your choice."

Filled with the Divine Spirit's confidence, Emma turned and walked toward the old auditorium. As they murmured, she sensed some people trailing behind her. When she arrived at the main entrance of the old auditorium, she turned to speak to the people who had followed her. To her delight, they were all there. Barney too. That's when Emma noticed Scarlett Steele and her cameraman, capturing everything on video.

Emma lifted her arms up and out at her sides to

get the people's attention. "We've been working hard this week to get the old auditorium ready for services—traditional services, just like you had twenty years ago and just like you want to see resumed. We had a practice service yesterday and today is our soft launch. Though it won't officially begin until next Sunday, you're welcome to come in today and see our progress. All I ask is that you offer us grace because we're still fine-tuning everything."

At that moment, Gavin walked out the front doors of the auditorium and stood next to Emma. "Please, come and join us." He gestured to the entrance. "Then stick around after the service and let us know what you think." Gavin turned around and opened the left door into the auditorium. Emma opened the right. The people filed in, with Barney leading the way.

Once everyone was inside, Scarlett hustled up to Emma, with microphone in hand. "Emma, this is exciting news. It seems you're giving them exactly what they have asked for. Does this mean you're rethinking the reforms you've been making to the Sunday services?"

"That's a great question, Scarlett. I appreciate you asking. The reforms we're doing are important. We must push forward to better align our practices with what the Holy Text says. Yet we also want to give options to people who aren't comfortable with that. Some people like the old ways. They like the old hymns, and they enjoy hearing the pipe organ. We'll give them all that each Sunday here in the old auditorium."

Scarlett lowered her microphone and the red light on the camera went out. "I know you probably don't want us recording the service," Scarlett said, "but could you make an exception for today? Please?"

"Just for today," Emma answered, "but stay in the back and don't distract from the service. If you want to talk to people afterward, you can do that outside as they leave. Also, remember this is a practice service. Please mention that in your coverage."

Scarlett asked Emma a couple more questions to round out her piece. "This afternoon, I'll put the story together to air on the evening news."

Emma thanked Scarlett with a quick hug and excused herself. She needed to hurry back to the new auditorium. She had no idea what kind of havoc her quick exit had caused or what she might encounter when she returned.

23

NO DISRESPECT INTENDED

Emma jogged back to the new auditorium as best as she could. She wasn't a jogger, and her priestly robe presented quite a challenge when she tried to run. Yet she pushed forward, bursting into the new auditorium, out of breath and flustered. She arrived more loudly than she wanted. Some people turned around to see the cause of the commotion. Yet they weren't glaring. If anything, they were concerned. There was no pandemonium as she feared might've happened after she walked out on them. And it didn't look like anyone had walked out of the service either.

She slowed her pace and stepped toward the main aisle, asking the Sovereign for peace and wisdom as she moved forward, all the while trying to catch her breath.

Mark stood at the dais. He extended his hands out and upward. "Please rise to receive your parting blessing." That's when he noticed Emma. He lowered his arms and smiled at those gathered. "I see the High Priestess has returned. If she wants, she can give today's concluding blessing."

Emma nodded to Mark as everyone turned around to gawk at her. With confidence, she glided toward the stage. If she'd been wearing sneakers and shorts, she'd have leapt onto it; she was sure she could have made it. Well, almost sure. But wearing her robe and with a thousand people watching—along with all those online—she decided not to try. She walked to the side of the stage and ascended the steps. As she approached the dais, Mark stepped aside and gestured toward it.

Taking a deep breath, Emma held out her hands to give them the blessing. Then she lowered them and turned on her mic. She paused as she scanned the crowd. "If you'd like to hear what just happened, have a seat. Otherwise, feel free to leave."

No one left. Everyone sat.

"As you saw when you arrived this morning, we

had a small group of protesters outside. They don't like the reforms we're making here and want to return to the way things used to be. In the middle of my message, the Sovereign told me to go out and talk with them. To do it right away and not wait for the service to end.

"I worried that would be disrespectful to you to leave in the middle of my teaching, but I realized it would be more disrespectful to the Sovereign if I stayed. I needed to obey the Sovereign, just like Talia did in today's text."

Emma paused and brought her hand to her chin. "What you don't know is that this week we've been readying the old auditorium to hold traditional services there. Much of our staff, some priests, and many volunteers have worked hard to make that happen. We got input from people to see what they liked about the old services. First was the pipe organ. Second was the choir and the old hymns. Third was the rhythm of the rituals that occurred throughout the service.

"We're bringing them all back . . . to the old auditorium. But we'll stay on track here to better align our Sunday practices with what we read in Scripture. Yesterday we held a practice service in the old auditorium. This morning we're having a soft launch. One of our lead priests, Gavin, is heading this up. He's doing an excellent job, and I'm sure everyone who wants a traditional service will be quite pleased.

"When you leave today, I doubt you'll see any protesters outside. That's because they're all at the old auditorium experiencing a traditional service, just like we did some twenty years ago." Emma grinned. "At least what I understand we did. I wasn't around then."

Then Emma remembered her lesson about Talia. Though there wasn't time for her to finish it, she needed to not leave the people hanging. "To learn what happened to Talia, read History 117 and 118. Or you can listen to the next service online. I hope I can finish my teaching then."

She lifted her arms to her sides and raised them heavenward. "Please stand to receive the parting blessing. Sovereign, we praise you for all you're doing here on the Temple grounds, for the reforms we're making, and for the options we're providing. Bless us as we move forward in these services and bless all the people as they move forward through their week. Bring us all back safely next Sunday. Amen."

24

UNWELL

On Monday morning, Emma was still basking in all the Sovereign had done on Sunday. The protesters had experienced the traditional service they wanted. The people in the new auditorium had extended grace to her for leaving in the middle of the service. And the second service celebrated all that happened that morning.

Yet the bounce in her step diminished as she neared the old Temple school. She heard chanting, but not as loudly as before. The protesters had returned. Their message was different, but even more hurtful.

"Emma Barlow is not a High Priest," they chanted. "Emma Barlow is a heretic."

Today there were only seven protesters, all priests—the remaining priests in Alpha group. She half expected to see Barney there encouraging them, but he was absent.

"Emma Barlow is not a High Priest. Emma Barlow is a heretic."

Today Emma was determined to talk to the malcontent priests. She walked up to them as they filed by. Then one of them broke rank and marched on the other side of her. The other priests followed him. Now the protesters surrounded her. They continued their chant.

"Emma Barlow is not a High Priest. Emma Barlow is a heretic."

"Can we talk?" Emma asked, trying to shout over them. "What's your real issue with me?"

As one of the protesting priests marched by, he paused his chant and hissed. "Reinstate the bonus program, and don't take back what we've rightfully earned." Then he resumed his chant, along with the other priests.

"Emma Barlow is not a High Priest. Emma Barlow is a heretic."

"The bonus program was illegal and unethical," Emma called out. "We had to stop it." She wasn't sure if any of them heard. She certainly knew they didn't care. "This is your last chance," she screamed. Then she lunged forward to break free of the rotating circle that held her captive, but they stretched out their hands to stop her. She was stuck.

"Help me, Sovereign!" Emma called out.

At that moment, the front door of the old Temple school building burst open. Out sped Joshua, with Chloe and Lane right behind him. The rest of her disciples streamed after them. As the group neared, the protesters stopped marching. She lunged forward to break free. This time the priests didn't stop her. Joshua caught Emma as she stumbled forward.

The priests resumed their chanting. "Emma Barlow is not a High Priest. Emma Barlow is a heretic."

"Thanks for rescuing me," she said to her disciples. Then she gazed up at Joshua, her eyes brimming with appreciation.

"The Sovereign told me you were in trouble and to come out here to help you."

"But I had just prayed for help when you showed up." Emma paused. Her gaze darted to her right. "I wonder if the Sovereign answered my prayer before I even asked?"

"Could be," Joshua said.

As Emma and her disciples entered the building, Emma glanced back at the protesters. That's when she noticed the Xtend News Network van parked behind them, with the cameraman recording everything.

Emma thanked the Sovereign for protecting her and keeping her safe. She prayed for supernatural peace to flow into her soul. She asked that she could focus on school and not fixate on the priests and their irritating protest.

When they reached their classroom, Emma turned to face her disciples. "Lane says he wants to be a priest. Do you all want to be priests? Is that why you're here?" She examined the twelve, peering deep into their eyes. Each one confirmed what Lane had told her. They all wanted to be priests.

"I'll do whatever I can to help. I'll work with Jennifer to come up with a workable plan. I doubt the Sovereign cares if you have seven years of college or went to seminary, just as long as you're spiritually ready for the work."

Emma remembered one more thing. "By the way, as I understand the Holy Text, there's nothing that says women can't be priests today. That door is now open."

As they filed inside the classroom, one by one, the six girls thanked Emma. After they passed by, she pulled out her phone to turn it off before school started. A text awaited her. It was from Barney. *I am unwell today and will not be in to work.*

He was up to something. Not only would he avoid her reprimand about his part in yesterday's protest, he also wouldn't be there if the police came to arrest the other priests.

25
——————

SEVEN

As they went to lunch, Emma's disciples buzzed about becoming priests, excited about what she had shared—especially knowing that it wouldn't take six or seven years of college. The twelve got their food and huddled to talk about it.

Emma met with her team for their regular working lunch.

Gavin joined them today. "Everything went off without a hitch at yesterday's traditional service," he reported. "When it was over, no one left. Everyone stayed, and we had a robust discussion. They were all so excited. Though we have a couple of tweaks to make for next Sunday, we'll be ready." Then

Gavin fixed his gaze on Emma. "Thank you for giving me this opportunity."

"I just opened the door," Emma said. "You walked through it and made the most of it."

"The staff who attended the service were excited as well," Christopher added. "I'm also pleased to announce the hiring of two new employees. Elizabeth Butler to teach the Holy Text, and David Hernandez to head up security. You'll meet Elizabeth later this week and David will join us shortly for an update. But he prefers we call him Hernandez."

Emma chuckled. Everyone looked at her, and she felt a need to explain. "To me, it's Mrs. Butler and Captain Hernandez."

Fred gave his update next. "In case you didn't catch it, Scarlett Steele's coverage of us on the evening news was most positive. She and Emma seem to have a great connection. We should continue to tap into it. Xtend News Network also recorded the service and asks permission to post it online in its entirety. Ordinarily I'd say 'no,' but this is a newsworthy event, and I'd like them to share it. Does anyone have concerns?"

"I'd like it posted too," Emma said. "But just

this once. I hope we can one day stream it, just like our other service."

"That's the plan," Gavin said. "Lane offered to help with the technical side of it."

Fred continued his update. "I understand the police plan to arrest the seven priests this afternoon, along with Barney Clark." Then Fred glanced around. "Where is he?"

Emma shook her head. "He called in sick. He says he's 'unwell'," she said as she made air quotes.

"That's an interesting development," said Hernandez as he approached the table with his food. "I understand some last-minute issues have arisen, so the arrests probably won't happen until late this afternoon, but they will happen."

He glanced at Fred. "Should I give the rest of my report now?"

Fred nodded.

"I've spent the morning scanning for bugs—for electronic listening devices. So far, I've found one in Emma's office, one in the small meeting room next to her office, and two in the conference room. I also found one in my office, as well as Frederick's."

Hernandez stood. "I should also scan each one of you before we say anything more. Put your phones and anything electronic on the table. Then stand up." He pulled out a device and passed it over each person as he walked around the group. "Good news. You're all clean. But I still have Mark's and Christopher's offices to check."

"With that," Fred said, "I'll adjourn our meeting. Once we can confirm the arrests, we'll let you know."

After lunch, Hernandez went to check Emma's room for bugs. He didn't find any. She was relieved. He didn't think there'd be any in their classroom, but they headed there to check it next, just to be sure. Jennifer's desk was clean and so was the area where the students normally sat.

Emma pointed to the back corner of the room, where Barney's copy of the Holy Text lay at his usual spot. It also checked out, but Hernandez noticed a bulge in the protective case. When he investigated, he pulled out four bugs. He studied them. "It doesn't look like they've been activated, but I'll quarantine them just the same." He pulled out his plastic vial, which was now half full of bugs, and added these to his collection. "Though it's circumstantial, I'm convinced Barney's the one planting the bugs."

Emma and Hernandez walked toward the main doors of the building. The seven priests were still protesting outside. The Xtend News Network van was still there too. As Emma and Hernandez watched, four squad cars and a police van sped into the parking lot and zoomed up to the priests. Within seconds, the police arrested, handcuffed, and carted away the seven fanatics. Xtend News Network videotaped the entire thing.

The detective who coordinated the arrests approached Hernandez. "This is the extent of our arrests. Our delay occurred because Barney Clark's legal team negotiated hard all morning, and we cut a deal. He will avoid arrest and prosecution with the agreement that he'll return most of the money he embezzled. It's looking to be about 35 million. The rest is either tied up in real estate or was used as hush money, though we can't prove that conclusively."

As he walked away, Scarlett and her cameraman approached the detective for an interview. He answered her questions and then excused himself. "I have a mountain of paperwork to process."

As he left, Scarlett approached Emma. "We featured this morning's incident with you and the priests on our noon news coverage. It's clear you tried to talk to them, and they physically restrained you. Are you open to record some sound bites for tonight's coverage of their arrest?"

Emma nodded, and the reporter lifted her microphone. The cameraman cued her. "Scarlett Steele here with Xtend News Network. We just witnessed the exciting arrest of the seven dissident priests, the fanatics who have opposed the High Priestess ever since she arrived. I understand they were arrested for conspiracy, fraud, and receiving stolen property, all relating to the illegal and unsanctioned bonuses they received over the past several years."

Scarlett turned to Emma. "Emma, as we covered in recent days, these priests have opposed you and given you a lot of grief. Yet through it all, you remained committed to finding a solution. But they rejected you each time. Are you glad this is finally over?"

"I appreciate the question. It's a bittersweet moment. I had hoped—and I had prayed—that they would come around. I wanted to work with them and help them become all they could be, just as we're doing with the other forty-one priests here and all the staff."

"You certainly gave them a lot of chances."

"Yes, I tried to talk to them many times," Emma

said, "but they were never interested. Their arrest ends their chance to be priests, but I'll pray for them, that they find a positive way to affect the world."

"They're all facing lengthy prison sentences," Scarlett said. "How could anything positive come from that?"

"With the Sovereign, anything is possible."

26

THREE STRIKES

When Scarlett and her cameraman left, Emma turned to Hernandez. "I guess we just struck out as far as Barney is concerned."

"These were our three best chances to put him away," Hernandez confirmed. "First, with the four women, then with the palace security guards, and now with the embezzled funds. But he weaseled his way out of each one. Yet they cost him dearly, especially this last time."

"I guess Frederick and I need to figure out what to do," Emma said. "I'm tired of Barney being my aide. Sometimes he's helpful, but other times he's stabbing me in the back."

Hernandez held up his hand. "Though it's a

longshot, we have one remaining chance. There's still the open investigation into him trying to poison you. The server says she was following his orders, but he claims she acted alone. It's her word against his, so it's going to be hard to get a conviction."

Emma's face lit up. "With all the other drama, I completely forgot, but I have a recording that should help."

She pulled out her phone and began searching. "At least I hope I still have it."

At last, Emma found the file and let out a relieved sigh. "When he had me poisoned and thought I was about to die, he came into my bedroom in the High Priest's residence. He pretty much confessed, but the recording is muffled. I'll jump to the good part."

Emma slid the progress button of the app forward and pressed play. She held up the phone for Hernandez to hear Barney's words:

The last High Priest lingered on in agony for months. Interestingly, a miscommunication between me and your server will cut yours short. When I told her to increase the dosage two times, she thought I said ten. It's kind of ironic. Frankly, I'm surprised you've made it this long.

Emma stopped the recording. "There's more, but I think that's the important part."

"It also raises questions about the death of your predecessor," Hernandez said. "Send me a copy of the recording right away. I'll pass it on to the detective. This might be the break we need."

27

LAST CHANCE

Emma strolled to school on Tuesday, relieved to not hear the chants of the protesting priests assaulting her ears. Quiet was good. She arrived early, surprised to see Mrs. Butler. "I thought you weren't a morning person!"

"I'm not." Mrs. Butler yawned. "My normal day will start at eleven and go till eight. But today I want to experience your microschool. It's a new concept for me, and I'm excited to witness how it functions."

"We had a couple rough days at the start as Jennifer fine-tuned it, but now it works great. It's so much better than regular school."

"I also wanted to let you know that when word

got out that I'd resigned my teaching position, a lot of homeschool parents asked me to teach their children about the Holy Text. I wonder if that's something I can add to my job here."

"If you want to teach in person, we have three more classrooms just like this one," Emma said. "We just need to get one cleaned up. If you want to teach online, we can work toward that too. Lane can help. Just add it to your plan for Christopher. You have my backing."

Barney arrived and slunk to his corner spot in the back. Staring at the ground, he avoided looking at Emma. Montgomery padded in at his side. He looked at Emma and wagged his tail.

"That man looks familiar," Mrs. Butler whispered.

"That's Barney Clark. He made everyone call him 'Your Royal Eminence.' He used to run this place—or at least he tried to."

"Oh. I've never seen him in person."

"Now he's my aide."

Mrs. Butler's eyebrows rose. "Keep your guard up. Don't trust him for a minute."

"You're so right," Emma said. "His spirit shines a glossy black. He's full of evil."

With Jennifer's permission, Mrs. Butler opened

the day explaining how their module about the Holy Text would work. Everyone was excited, and they embraced their studies for the day.

As usual, Emma finished her work first. Instead of waiting for Joshua and Chloe, she quietly left. Hernandez awaited her outside. He held up his hand to stop Barney from getting any closer. "A quick update," he whispered. "The detective has enough evidence to make an arrest. It should happen later today. Until then, I'm going to stay at your side."

"Not necessary," Emma said. "The Sovereign will protect me."

"I admire your faith, but permit me to help."

Hernandez signaled that Barney could now approach. The three headed to the cafeteria.

At lunch, the discussion centered on all the money they'd recovered from the priests returning their illegal bonuses. It was enough to pursue all the needed capital improvements: the ancient Temple, the Temple school dorm rooms, and the lower level of the priests' quarters. They also had the lead remediation issue in the palace and a few minor repairs in the old auditorium to do.

Now they could address them all. They

discussed how to move ahead in the most effective way possible.

After lunch, Emma headed to her new office in the palace. She wanted to spend some time organizing it before her afternoon meetings began. As promised, Hernandez walked at her side. Barney and Montgomery followed.

The afternoon sun warmed her walk, while a gentle breeze kept her comfortable. Peace flowed into Emma's spirit. She wanted to slow down and enjoy the Sovereign's creation, yet another part urged her to hurry to her office and make it her own.

Interrupting her thoughts came the sirens of two police cars. They skidded to a stop right in front of her. Two officers jumped out of each one and rushed toward them. "Barney Clark, you're under arrest for murder, attempted murder, conspiracy, and bribery."

"Emma," Barney called out, "stop this madness. It's all a misunderstanding. Save me."

She shook her head. He deserved justice, not mercy. An officer cuffed Barney's wrists behind his back.

"Please, Emma!" Barney begged. The officer tugged at Barney's arm to spin him around and haul him away. The other three officers surrounded him and herded him toward the squad cars. Barney twisted his neck to peer at her. "Emma! Attend to Montgomery. He's all I have left."

Emma kneeled and clapped her hands. "Come here, Montgomery."

His ears perked up, and he looked at her.

"Come here, boy." Emma slapped her thigh.

Montgomery raced toward her, running faster than she'd ever seen him move.

If you enjoyed *Fighting the Fanatics*, please leave a review online. Your review will help others learn about this book and encourage them to read it too.

Thank you.

PERFECTING THE PRIESTHOOD

BOOK 7 IN THE NEXT HIGH PRIEST SERIES

Chapter 1: A Fresh Start

Emma watched the officers lead the handcuffed Barney Clark away. This time he'd be gone for good. She knew that for sure. The Sovereign had told her.

Between her feet stood a trembling Montgomery. The tiny puppy's tail was tucked tightly between his rear legs. He whimpered at the sight of his master being hauled away.

"I think we're finally rid of him," said Fred, Emma's executive admin. Then he glanced at her and cocked his head to the side. "You're not about to cry, are you?"

Emma shook her head. "No. I just wonder how things might have turned out had he made better decisions. When he wasn't scheming behind my back, he was a good aide. Quite good."

"We can certainly find you another aide."

"I don't need one. I've got you and the rest of the team to help me in my role here at the Temple as High Priestess. We made up the aide position just so we could keep tabs on him. I'm more worried about Montgomery. He doesn't understand what just happened, but he knows it was something bad. He's terrified. Just look at him shaking."

As Fred glanced at Montgomery, cowering between Emma's feet, she bent down and scooped up the tiny pup. "It's okay, little buddy. I'll take care of you. Don't worry."

"From the beginning, he's taken a shine to you," Fred said. "So you've got that going for you, but what do you know about taking care of dogs?"

"Not much," Emma admitted. "But I know just who can help." She ruffled the fur on Montgomery's head, and he received her affection with delight, his tail wagging for the first time since his master had been carted off. "Let's go visit Auntie Ashley."

Fred shook his head. "Auntie Ashley?"

Emma giggled. "Maybe I'm more of a dog person than I realized." Emma lowered Montgomery to the ground and turned to go visit the cosmetologist. Montgomery trotted along beside her, his head bobbing with each step.

Emma reached the salon and opened the door. Angie—who had helped Emma free the prisoners—sat in the chair with Ashley standing next to her. Startled, they stopped talking and froze. Ashley turned red, while Angie's face blanched. They both stared at Emma, unblinking.

"Sorry to interrupt," Emma said. "I'll try later." She stepped back, but Ashley stopped her. "No worries. We're done. Just having some girl talk."

Emma studied each woman. Angie was almost old enough to be Ashley's grandmother. What would a seasoned nurse have in common with a 19-year-old cosmetologist? Emma waited for Ashley to say more, something the young woman excelled at, but she remained silent. Emma had definitely interrupted something important.

Angie stood. "I was just leaving," she said to Emma. Then she turned to Ashley. "We'll talk more later." She gave Ashley a sly wink. Then the amiable nurse left the salon.

That's when Ashley noticed Montgomery. "Oh!

How exciting." Ashley bounced on her toes as she clapped her hands. "You brought your little friend with you." Ashley bent down to welcome Montgomery, and he bounded up to her. "Would you like a little puppy treat? Sure you do. Let me get you something special." She turned and stepped into her storage room, returning with something cupped in her hand. Montgomery smelled it right away. He looked up at her with expectation, his tail thumping on the floor. Ashley held out her hand to him and opened it. Montgomery lunged forward and lapped up his treat.

When Ashley looked up, Emma explained. "They arrested Barney this morning, and we're finally rid of him."

"About time," Ashley said. "Oops. Shouldn't have said that. Pretend you didn't hear it."

"The last thing he said before they hauled him away," Emma said, "was 'Attend to Montgomery. He's all I have left.' So I now have a dog to care for. I figured you'd be the best person to help me. Do you have a leash I can borrow?"

"Certainly." Ashley ducked into the room and returned with her bag of doggy things. She pulled out a leash and handed it to Emma. She reached back in. "And you'll need these too."

"What are they?"

"Poop bags, of course."

Emma rolled her eyes. "Great."

Ashley rummaged through the bag. "Here's a longer leash too. You can keep everything. I won't be needing them."

"Why?" Emma asked. "I thought you wanted a dog."

"I did. But now it doesn't seem so important. When Topher and I get married, we want to start our family right away. A dog won't get much attention if we have a baby to care for."

Even though the cosmetologist was four years older, Emma viewed Ashley as a peer. The thought of her friend having a baby jarred her. Yet when she and Joshua got married, they might make the same decision. She shuddered at the thought.

Ashley pulled out a toy from the bag and squeaked it twice, tossing it into the corner of her shop. That's when Emma noticed the doggy bed still there in the corner. Montgomery bounded toward the squeaky toy, grabbed it in his mouth, and retreated to the bed. He snuggled down, his eyes darting between Emma and Ashley, as if waiting for one of them to say something.

"Be sure to keep him hydrated," Ashley said. "If

you're thirsty, he probably is too. And make sure he doesn't get overheated. When I'm done working, I'll help you get set up for tonight. I should have everything you need—I know I do. Even dog food."

Emma crouched to clip the short leash on Montgomery's collar. When she stood, he darted around her and stood at her right side.

Ashley's eyes sparkled. "Looks like someone's been to puppy school. You should check into that. Half of puppy school is training the owner."

The weight of being a puppy parent was looming large. So much responsibility. Emma wondered if she was ready for it.

Ashley agreed to meet Emma at her room shortly after five. Emma turned to leave.

"Tell him to heel," Ashley called out. "Say it with authority."

"Heel, Montgomery!" The puppy scooted up to Emma and walked along on her right side, his head held high and his tail wagging.

Emma held her head high, too, a pleased grin plastered on her face.

Her phone vibrated. She had a text. It wasn't anyone on her contact list. Puzzled, she read the message aloud, as if Montgomery needed to hear it.

"It's time for us to meet. Since you can't drive, I'll come to you. This Thursday at 3:00. —PM."

Who in the world is PM?

Continue this story in *Perfecting the Priesthood*, Book 7 of The Next High Priest Series.

ABOUT PETER DEHAAN

Peter DeHaan is an adult who dreams of being a teenager. When he's not contemplating grown-up thoughts, his mind retreats to the domain of invented worlds with his loyal and most real, yet still imaginary, friends. What grand adventures they have: righting wrongs, solving problems, and making their world a better place to live.

His first published adventures come to life in "The Next High Priest Series"—a faith-friendly speculative fiction adventure in a world just like ours . . . only different.

Next up is *The Curious Gift*, a YA contemporary novella with a hint of the supernatural.

Then comes "The Ice Creamed Series," a present-day quest for friendship and love, all the while trying to survive high school unscathed and ping-ponging between responsible impulses and irresponsible slipups.

Want more? Get a free short-story prequel about Emma along with news of upcoming books when you sign up to receive Peter's updates at PeterDeHaan.com/fiction.

FICTION BOOKS BY PETER DEHAAN

The Next High Priest Series

Seeking the Sovereign

Confronting the Chaos

Dueling the Devil

Reforming the Religion

Freeing the Prisoners

Fighting the Fanatics

Perfecting the Priesthood

Pursuing the Politicians

Restoring the Repentant

Learn more at PeterDeHaan.com/fiction.